POOR SUPERMAN!

You are an unsuspected superman.
You are a member of the new emerging race that
*   will one day rule the world.*
But the rest of your fellow supermen and women
*   are not so nice.*
They plan to conquer and enslave ordinary
*   human beings.*
And if you don't join them—they'll kill you!
There's no place on this world for you to hide.
But there is another world you've learned about,
*   one where you can hide and get time to think*
*   and plan.*
If you can get there.
And if you can survive when you do.
Poor superman.

"Ted White doesn't need dates and rocketships
and all the mechanical trappings to prove it's science
fiction."
—IF Magazine

"If any current science fiction writer has the
capacity to go mainstream, it's Ted White."
—Analog

D0555935

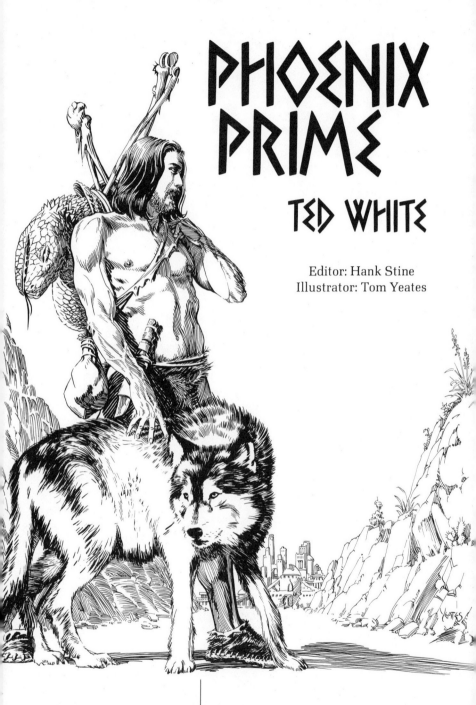

PHOENIX PRIME

TED WHITE

Editor: Hank Stine
Illustrator: Tom Yeates

STARBLAZE
EDITIONS

The Donning Company/Publishers
5659 Virginia Beach Boulevard
Norfolk, Virginia 23502

Library of Congress Cataloging in Publication Data

White, Ted.
    Phoenix prime.

    (The Star Wolf trilogy)
    I. Title. II. Series: White, Ted.
Star Wolf trilogy.
PS3573.H4749P5   1982   813'.54   82-12872
ISBN 0-89865-251-0

Printed in United States of America

DEDICATION
To Barbara—Remember?
and
To my daughter, Arielle
this time around

Chapter 1

He lived. He was aware. For the first time he was truly alive and aware. He was everything in his world. He—

He wrapped flames around his body, letting them pour sinuously around and over him. For a second, as he stood in the center of the floor, he writhed. It was pure reflex; then he relaxed and gave himself up to the heady luxury of the roaring fire which clothed his body. He basked in the flames.

His mind was afire, too. It was like—satin ice? No, those were words, and this was different, something new; his senses were still adjusting themselves to the new reality, and his mind contained no images with which to compare it. He didn't see or hear Fran open the door.

"*Max!*"

He shook his flaming body, and a few brief cinders fell away in sparks. Then, suddenly, he had snuffed out the aura of flames and was standing nude on a smoking carpet, grinning tentatively at the girl. He swallowed and said, "Hell of a time for you to show up, Fran."

She stared at him without expression, looking up at him with almost unseeing eyes, her face taut, skin unnaturally white.

He blinked, slowly coming down or up to reality again. Good God, yes, she thought he'd been burning up. The odor of the burnt carpet—it smelled like scorching hair.

"I forgot about the carpet." He watched her glance down at it. Acrid smoke still curled away from two singed-bare and smoldering patches where he'd been standing. Without thinking, he turned his gaze upward. Yes, the paint on the ceiling was blistered, too. He'd have to be more careful with such stunts in the future.

When he looked back down at her, Fran's eyes were on his. She said, "Max—!"

She took one faltering step toward him; then she crumpled and swayed forward. He caught her in his arms as she fell, straining her close. The physical contact of their bodies brought him completely back, made him truly aware of Fran's plight— and, of Fran.

He tried to make his grip as firm, as reassuring as he could— to bring her back to a world in which men were not, one minute, cloaked in streaming flame, and the next minute alive and human and—

"Max!" She straightened with a hysterical giggle. "You don't have any *clothes* on!"

"I know. I lose more pajamas that way," he said, lightly, keeping his voice casual. The light touch, take it easy, he cautioned himself. You've given this girl quite a shock. "Can you hold on for a moment, Fran? Sit down and I'll put on a pair of pants, at least."

Her face was chalk-white; the color had drained from her mouth, leaving the lipstick like paint on a corpse. She was rigid with shock. She hardly seemed to hear him, and let him lead her, like a child, to the sofa. *God in heaven, why did she have to come in just then?*

"Lie down here for a minute, Fran. Here, put your feet up on the arm. Fran, it's all right, I'm all right; take it easy now. I'll be right back."

He retreated into the bedroom, quietly closed the door behind him, and leaned against it for a moment. His whole body slumped.

It would be so easy—so easy, just to forget, to forget it all. Two paths branched out before him, and he was at the fork. Which should be his turning? In one direction, normalcy, safety. In the other—what?

But there could be only one answer. His life had changed, had been changed, and now he had changed another's life. There could be no negating that.

The room was quiet, just a third-floor bedroom in an old house, now a converted rooming house for students presided over by an old spinster for whose long-dead family this had once been a proud town-house. The room was papered with flowers and butterflies, fading in the strong sunlight which now half filled it. Max heard his own breathing loud in the silence, looked down at his naked body, then at his pants, draped over the bed. He stared at them and closed his eyes. His body grew tense and rigid.

2

Slowly, the pants began to stir as if were a breeze—but all else was still. Sunlight cut across the stationary dustmotes suspended in mid-air, and the warm summer afternoon seemed to hold its breath. The pants legs flapped.

Then, suddenly, the room was filled with a timeless density. The silence of the moment before thickened into a tangible, measurable dimension, possessing a reality of its own. He could taste it.

He rose three feet into the air, his head clearing the ceiling by inches. As he did so, the tension dissolved from his muscles; he lay loose-flung in the air and watched articles of clothing—first his briefs, then pants, sweatshirt, socks, and finally shoes—moving to him and draping themselves over, around, up and onto his body, flowing onto him as if themselves fluid.

The door opened before he reached it. He took a deep breath, set his feet on the floor, and walked through the door. Behind him it was as if the sheerest soap bubble had burst.

Fran started upright as he came in, and flinched away.

"Fran, are you afraid of me?"

She nodded, moving her mouth mutely.

Easy, now.

"Afraid of *me?* Even with my clothes on and no attempt at felonious assault?"

"Don't laugh," she said, finding her voice. "Please. I know what you're trying to do. But—don't. And don't try to tell me that I didn't see—what I saw." Her eyes moved quickly, a little rabbit movement, to the charred carpet, and away again.

"Fran." He seated himself beside her and took her face in his hands. "I'm not going to deny anything. I'm not going to try to talk you out of anything. What you saw—it happened, yes. Would you like to know *how* it happened?"

"Then I'm not crazy? It wasn't all—an illusion?"

"No. And I'm not a warlock, or a weaver of dark spells, and I haven't sold my soul to the devil. Okay?" His eyes twinkled. At least he hoped they did.

She smiled up at him, a faint and tentative smile, but none the less a genuine smile. She raised her hand to his, caught it, and pulled him down until they were lying side by side.

Touch did what words had only attempted; he felt the rigid frozen fright flow out of her as she held him. With a sigh, she snuggled close against his chest, nesting inside the sweep of his reassuring arm.

Affirmation, a reassurance of that which held them, the spirit that existed between them. It was important, he knew, that she

3

understand that nothing had *really* changed—not between them. This was the best way. It had come to him without words; perhaps there were no words. But what had he done to Fran, to this shy girl who clung to him so tightly? He sensed, through the tension of her terror and it release, that she still loved him—did he still return that love? It was important that she think that— that she know that. But did he? How far had the changes gone? When he asked himself this, he could not answer—yet, now, in his response to her, he sensed his answer.

Words, mere words—what did they mean? Reasoning could be a barrier instead of a path. He had always felt most apart from Fran when he had tried to think out their relationship into words. Better to let the words go, better to react.

They lay together unmoving on the sofa for a moment which was, for them, timeless—perhaps fifteen minutes, perhaps two or three hours. Time was a dimension away from which Max had drifted increasingly. They exchanged no words, no gestures, not even a kiss. They simply *were*, sharing a moment of that meshed, tangible silence in which there was no Max, no Fran; instead a gestalt, a separate and whole emotional entity.

"Tell me about it," she said finally.

It was like surfacing after a deep dive. He blinked. "I don't know what happened."

"How did it begin?"

He shifted slightly, turning so that he faced her, looking down into her upward-tilted face and searching eyes. He paused, then reached out for words and found them.

"If you want to be rational about it—that is, if we *can* be rational about it—I guess it's what they call a wild talent."

"*Wild* is right," she said with a shaky laugh.

"Psi power, I guess you'd call it, then. I can make things— happen.

"I had a dream last night. It was a very strange kind of dream—you know how sometimes you have dreams about flying? Like, you're running along on the ground, and sometimes you can jump, and pull your feet up, into the air, and then you sort of paddle yourself along with your hands, as though you were swimming—? I dreamed I'd done this and I was floating and weightless, pulling myself around with handholds like an astronaut in a space capsule, only the handholds were the branches of a tree. I was floating and pulling myself into the tree.

"Things began feeling strange. Like two images super-imposed—like things were happening in double. The dream was

fading, the way it does when you're sleepwalking, and you're aware of both your dream surroundings and your real ones simultaneously.

"Then I woke up.

"Fran, *I was holding on to the curtains of the window next to my bed, and I was floating about even with the top of the open window!*"

He felt her arms tighten their grasp on him, but she did not interrupt. He went on:

"It scared me silly, but in a very practical sort of way. My first thought was, *My God, I nearly went out the window*—just as matter of factly as if I'd been sleepwalking and woke up and said, *Oh, I almost fell down those stairs.* And then I guess I woke up the rest of the way and realized what was really happening, because the next thing I knew, I was lying crossways on the bed with all the breath knocked out of me."

Her body had tensed again with the growing excitement of his voice. He felt her shiver. "Fran, don't worry. I'm not going to do anything now."

Slowly, under the reassurance of his voice and touch, he felt her spasm dissolve, and he continued, speaking with careful gentleness.

"When I woke up again this morning, I thought it had all been a dream. Or rather, I wanted to believe I'd dreamed it, but I knew better.

"I wandered out here into the living room, and just kind of went through the motions of breakfast, without noticing what I was doing. I remember at one point I looked at my watch and saw that it was already nine-thirty. I thought of calling in and reporting sick, but it didn't seem important enough to bother.

"After a while I—well, located myself. I was sitting at the table, staring at my coffee and realizing it had gone cold. I wasn't really thinking about anything. I was just staring at that coffee and wishing it was good and hot again, and—then it started *steaming*.

"I didn't touch it. I just looked at it. It seemed important to me that I really look at it—and then suddenly I wasn't just looking at a cup of coffee any more. I was *seeing* it—*really* seeing it. I stopped looking at it as a familiar object, a sort of stereotyped object which represents a set of symbols neatly filed in my mind with the proper non-thinking associations. People take everything familiar for granted. Fran, and so had I.

"Until then. Then I began discarding all the cardboard facades which spell out *cuppacawfee,* and I began to see the relationships of each and every component in the cup and the coffee, the chemical and molecular relationships and deeper. I don't have the words for what I saw, but I could sort of *grasp,* not really seeing, using my eyes at all—I felt the entire series of relationships between all the overlapping fields of energy, or—" He stopped, uncertainly.

"Damn words, anyway. I'm trying to make sense of it for you, and I'm not even making sense to myself.

"Look. Everything is really *motion.* I can't pin it down any better than that, but I could see—sense—the fact that the cup and the coffee were really fields of motion. Sort of webworks, finely woven, very intricate, like twisted paths of light. Like—yeah, like those time exposures of cars and lights on the streets at night; all those lights all woven together to create the whole, the identity which we label 'coffee' or 'cup.'

"I saw that motion, and I knew that I could reach out and— speed it up, or slow it down. I'd done that. I'd heated up the coffee.

"I was fascinated. I started looking around me, looking at everything. First I looked at little things, individual objects. It was like putting them under a microscope and finding out what they were really like. I'd pick something up, and look at it. I spent what must have been an hour at least on my transistor radio. I just couldn't help admiring it, admiring the lovely intricacy of it all. Those transistors and diodes—just lovely!

"It was like double vision, a second sight. I could turn it on and off. I could make it overlap my normal vision, or supplant it. The funny thing was, I discovered that I could function on my new sense equally well. I could look at the whole room that way, ignoring the minute patterns and seeing the larger ones. In a way, it blended right in with normal sight. I mean, have you ever really just *looked* at things? If you stop just glancing over all the familiar objects, and look at a room as though you'd never seen it before, it can be fascinating. You can make out all sorts of relationships, the rhythms of color, the placement of masses and empty areas, the similarities and clashes in the lines of different furniture—this place is a real hodgepodge—and you can see the whole room as a three-dimensional area, an integrated whole."

She was looking around her at the room, and he smiled to himself. The touch of the strange—that was what frightened her. Seeing the familiar as a shaky bunch of colored wires was a terrifyingly alien concept, but looking at an old furnished room as a problem in design appealed to the interior decorator in her. She was familiar with Zen, she'd read Watts on Tao. This concept of integration, of everything being part of a larger pattern, was something she could grasp and understand.

"I haven't really tried anything yet. I haven't even explored much more than that. I've been a little afraid to really try much, because it smacks of playing God, so I've been piddling with parlor tricks. I'm sorry you had to walk in on one cold like that, Fran. It was such a childish stunt for me to pull."

"What—what was it like?"

"It was ego-inflating, basically. Very wild and weird, you know. The Human Torch and all that. I turned the air around myself to flames—and burned off my pajamas before I'd thought to protect more than my body. I've done some other cute stunts, too. I've levitated, and wished my clothes on, and moved things around—but those are such *little* things. Petty things. Mainly because I haven't really wanted to face the fact that I could do so much more than that if I wished."

Fran pulled away from him and pushed herself up to a sitting position. He stood up and stretched. The odor of scorched carpeting was almost gone; a gentle breeze wafted freshly through the windows. The air seemed clean and empty. Fran smiled up at him.

"Thanks, Max." She took his hand and pulled herself to her feet, standing close by him. "What are you going to do now?"

"I wish I knew," he answered slowly. "I wish I knew how I'd

come by all this, and what I ought to do with it. It—it takes in a lot of territory, you know. I don't even know how far I can extend it, just how much I can do with it." He frowned and shook his head, as if to clear it.

"Perhaps I can help," she said, still holding his hand.

He smiled down at her, now sure in his love for her. "Perhaps you can," he said.

Chapter 2

They lay on their backs in the grass, their fingers intertwined, staring up into the summer sky. Low-hanging clouds were moving majestically out of the west, and the air hung heavily in the warm yellow sunlight.

Nearby, a squirrel chattered in annoyance. The focus of its attention, a pigeon, was pecking at an open bag of peanuts at the edge of the grass. A heavy-set woman dressed as a nurse slowly pushed a baby carriage along the paved path, pausing frequently to mop her florid face. In the distance there was the faint but solid sound of a baseball bat cracking out a hit, and, farther away, the muted roar of the city. The air smelled sweetly of freshly mown grass.

The squirrel turned at the sight of the woman with the baby carriage and ran chattering in anger up the nearest tree, then slipped back down again, returning in her wake to the now unguarded peanuts.

Maximillion Quest was a young man, young enough to still sometimes be mistaken for a college student. That he was not was due to two circumstances of his life. The first was the death of his parents in a plane crash when he was seventeen. The second was his lack of any interest in an academic education. In the six years which had followed his parents' death, he had worked as a stock boy for a book wholesaler, as a longshoreman, as the manager of a village coffee house, and, most recently, as a taxi driver. He sometimes joked that he would need only to work as a shoe salesman before becoming a bestselling novelist.

He had a tall, well-filled body, onto which his occupational labors had built a good set of muscles. His features were slightly rough-hewn, rugged in a not-unpleasing fashion, giving him an honest and open look. While he was far from handsome in the traditional matinee-idol fashion, women sometimes referred to his "dark good looks"—this largely during his coffee-house phase.

At times friends would ask him why he'd never tried to make more of himself, why he had not tried to finish high school and go on to college, so that he might "go places," as, by inference, they were doing. His reply was always a shrug and a smile, suggesting that perhaps that was not where he really wanted to go anyway. "I can't really believe in myself being one of those white-collar types, sitting behind a desk in some office," he'd once confessed to Fran. "I don't know where I'll end up, but wherever it is, it won't be in any neat little pigeonhole."

He liked working with his hands, liked jobs which left his mind free to roam other worlds. In a way, that was what had gone wrong with his career in the Village—it was too absorbing, and he'd become too involved with it. He hadn't ever really wanted to become involved that much with anything. In the end, of course, he'd come out of it unscathed: the coffee house had failed, as such establishments are wont to do, and he'd been freed once more.

Now he had only one real commitment in the world: Fran.

Their first meeting had been an accident of circumstances: she lived on the floor below his. The house they lived in was a typically narrow brownstone of the type common along the west border of Central Park in the middle seventies; once a reasonably well-to-do town house, it was now divided into small apartments, the only remnants of its former splendor the inlaid parquet floors still peeking in spots from under worn linoleum.

He'd met her one day as she was carrying out her garbage, and he'd helped her with it. It was hardly the "meet cute" of Hollywood, and while his practiced eye had found her attractive, he'd made no immediate moves toward her. But proximity had had its effects; six months later he found she was cooking dinners for him, and often spending her free afternoons in his empty apartment listening to records on his hi-fi.

That was the way it had gone; they'd fallen into their relationship easily and by degrees, without ever experiencing the sudden wrench of head-over-heels infatuation. Max, for his part, had been content to accept whatever might occur and found no need to push things. Fran, he sensed, held in her past a still-fresh wound, for she too preferred the gentle easiness of their gradual growing together to a more tumultuous kind of love.

Frances Towne, at twenty-one, was no longer the girlish beauty she'd been upon coming, naively and innocently, to the Big City. Experience had etched away youthful naivete, limning now her growth into womanhood.

She was small, but not quite petite. Dark hair was cut short, the close curls giving her a pixie look; taken with her slightly snubbed nose the effect was impish. Usually her outward disposition matched her appearance, and she was gay and vivacious. But now, Max knew, he had penetrated that shell, and might never be able to see her that way again.

"It would almost be easier if it would go away again," he said. Grass tickled the back of his neck, and with his free hand he raked the loose cuttings into a small nest. "There's so much to it, so much to think about. I don't even know where to start."

He picked some of the grass up and sprinkled it across her in mock baptism. "For instance, why should I work any more? I don't have to. I'm sure that one way or another I can have everything I need now—everything I want. But what do I want? All my life I've been looking for a way to live without the drudgery of working. Now I can do it. So what will I do? Besides lying on my back in the grass all the time, I mean."

"There's so much more you can do, though," Fran said, squeezing his hand. "Think of all the great problems of the world—hunger, overpopulation, war, disease—maybe you could do something about them!"

"You know," Max said, after a pause, "when I was a kid, I used to read comic books. I remember trading another kid for a whole bunch of World War II comics when I was ten or eleven. It was a big thrill for me; they were old treasures.

"That was a big war. I used to hear my father talking about the campaigns he fought in. It was a war vaster and more terrible than any before it. It was fought all over the world.

"Well, in among all these comics I'd gotten were some Superman comics. And here was Superman, fighting mobsters and mad scientists and all those petty types while this great war was going on. It didn't make sense to me. Why wasn't Superman fighting in that war, I used to wonder. He could've cleaned things up in nothing flat!

"It was a long time later, when I no longer even pretended to believe in comic book superheroes, that I realized what a tough spot his publishers had been in. They couldn't put him in the war since he did have all those super powers. If they had, we'd still be really fighting that war long after Superman had mopped it all up—and who'd believe in that? It was better to have him flunk his physical by seeing through the eye chart with his X-ray vision, and have some general say, 'With our men away, we need you to keep the home shores safe,' or something like that, and just keep him out of the real problems of the world.

"I'm Superman. I don't really know how vast my powers are—or just how vastly they can be applied. But here I am, in the real world, with comic-book powers. I can't really believe in it. All I need is a suit of red underwear and a cape and I'll flip out, you know?

"But one thing keeps bugging me. Why *me*? Why hasn't this ever happened to anyone before? And if it has, why haven't we already felt its effects?"

Fran had found a peanut in the grass and was holding it out to the squirrel. She gave it a little chr-r-r of invitation, and it began sidling toward her hesitantly, nose wriggling.

"It's too big, Max," she said. "Too big to just figure out. You'll just have to accept it for what it is, for now, and let yourself grow accustomed to it, until you can handle it easily."

The squirrel jumped back as Max turned on his side, leaned over Fran, and gave her a kiss. "You're right," he said. He settled back and let his attention wander once more to the panorama of the sky.

The sun had shifted behind one of the gathering banks of clouds, and Max stared up in wordless fascination at the boiling milky turbulence of the growing thunderhead. Almost like letting his eyes slip out of focus, he made the shift into his newfound second sight.

There was a sudden jarring change of perspective, almost like one of those Sunday-supplement optical illusions in which first the stairs or blocks seem to recede away from you and then suddenly they're coming up *toward* you, all because you suddenly begin looking at them in another way. Max had found another way.

At their forefront, no longer directly catching and reflecting the sunlight, the clouds looked, to the naked eye, coldly blue-white. But up beyond, in the canopy still exposed to the sun, Max discovered a crystal latticework of reflecting interstices, a trelliswork of energies, woven angular motion all glinting and darting. He moved his attention deeper, into the interior of the thundercloud, and there he found a dark fiery power, a compression and gathering of coiled forces which grew in intensity with every moment.

Suddenly a scream sliced sharply through his reverie, and he pulled himself back to ground and grass.

Still with his second sight, he turned his startled gaze upon Fran.

For a second he had the impression of total chaos. What he

Max stared up in wordless fascination at the boiling milky turbulence of the growing thunderhead.

saw before him made no sense: unresolved forces seemed to be pitched in random movements.

"*Max!*" Fran screamed again, and he brought the patterns into focus.

The squirrel had seized her wrist in its teeth and was gnawing at it! Even as he perceived this, Max launched himself at the animal, grabbing its head in one hand, his fingers prying the jaws apart, and wrenched it loose from Fran's profusely bleeding arm.

He was about to fling the maddened little beast from him when it squirmed about in his grasp, and, fierce claws ripping deeply into his wrists and hands, launched itself at his neck!

The sharp pain and shocking realization that the squirrel was *attacking* him jolted Max into an awareness of his other abilities, and in that timeless moment he cursed himself for forgetting so easily.

Time ebbed. An ear-numbing stillness settled over him, a pocket of motionlessness which protectively surrounded him. Twisted, writhing motionlessly through the air, the squirrel hung almost suspended a foot before him. Again, he reached out, but this time with his mind instead of his ripped and bleeding hands.

He touched the squirrel and it went limp. He looked *into* the animal, and found wrongness. It was indefinable, but there—an alien quality, a touch of imbalance. This was not a disease-maddened animal, but one which— It was nothing he could put his finger on, only something akin to that sense possessed by all good mechanics, who can listen to or look at a machine they've never seen before and detect a malfunction. The squirrel had been—*tampered* with.

He relaxed the mental tension which had held this hiatus in time and lowered the now lifeless body to the ground. He turned to Fran.

Her eyes were staring, wide and almost unseeing, at him. He reached out his hand and touched her. "Dear Fran. It's all right now; it's all right." The sudden senseless attack had caught her with her defenses down, and the apparent speed with which he'd handled it had left her no time for adjustment. There would have to be a way—

Suddenly the air was full of pulsation. Letting his paranormal vision slip momentarily, he looked up to see, descending upon them, a flock of pigeons.

Pigeons? For a moment he didn't understnad, and then he did. First the squirrel, now these. He stiffened, tensing the muscles of his mind like a fist.

14

Then the air was filled with flapping wings, scratching claws and snapping beaks. The birds were upon them.

His mind still a fist, he struck out. This time there was no hesitation, no pause to leisurely examine. He knew that if he looked into them he would find the same strange *disturbance*. Before they could touch Fran or him, he *exploded* at them, striking out with a fiercely unleashed force born of righteous anger which tore the birds apart, and flung them outwards, away from Fran and himself. The pigeons screamed, a weird, unearthly shriek, and then were gone. A few drifting feathers settled to the ground around them, mute evidence of the attack. Slowly, he unclenched himself.

Was this to be all? he wondered. Or would something more dangerous strike next?

His immediate answer was an incredible incandescence of the air about them, accompanied by a concussion so terrible that he felt himself disintegrating.

The survival pattern! His mind screamed with soundless agony, but he clung tenaciously. He must not relinquish that: so long as he could hold together the image of the very energy patterns of their bodies, they could not be destroyed. Flesh might be stripped from their bones and fried in the white heat of destruction, but if he could keep the pattern, if he could only hold them together, flesh and bone would be resimulated, regathered out of the primal atoms and life-energy of the cosmos—and they would still be whole.

He reorganized his pattern a little, and the tearing pain subsided; then he recreated substance.

They were standing in the center of a charred and devastated area which had only shortly before been covered with freshly cut grass. Now the air stank of ozone and was so charged that Max felt his hair standing stiffly upraised along his arms and on the back of his neck.

He didn't know if he could take that again. It was only pure good fortune which had lent him the strength to reach out in that one blazing fraction of a moment and seize hold of their life-patterns with an instinctive knowlege that it was their only chance. He had felt himself rent nearly apart, and now his strength, thrown away casually upon the earlier attacks, was nearly spent. The squirrel, the pigeons—he knew now they were only feints, designed to feel him out, draw him out, build up a false confidence in him which would leave him unprepared for the real attack when it came. He'd sensed it, building and growing, in that cloud above, and his attention had been cleverly diverted. Now,

15

now—

He'd thrown a protective canopy over them as soon as he'd reassembled them, and now his wisdom was proven. Within only a few seconds, barely pause enough for him to assess his surroundings, the stygian gloom which had followed the first thunderbolt was broken again by a second brilliant flash of lightning. This time a wall separated them from it, and they were only buffeted.

A third clap of thunder and bolt of lightning struck.

Was there to be no end? How much longer could he maintain his defenses? Putting his arm around the cowering girl beside him, he donned his second sight, and began to see—

Great snakes writhed upwards from the devastated ground around them, twisting skyward along invisible paths, boiling upward like an obscene waterspout.

They were at the focus, Max realized, and bounded in every direction by more than twenty feet.

The sparkling snakes climbed, wavered, climbed again, beckoning, always beckoning. And up above—

High above, from deep within the electrical cauldron of the thunderhead, answering tendrils groped downward, darting, reaching, in answer to the flicking tongues—

They touched. Suddenly there was a whole path, and then it was galvanized by a great surge of unbelievable energy.

They were like fish in a barrel. The ground surrounding them had been energized, given a high-voltage charge with which to attract the lightning bolts from the clouds above. And it was no happenstance, no freak accident. It was willed.

If it has been willed upon them, it could be willed away. It *had* to be. Max gathered his waning forces and reached out from his mind.

Like live snakes, these tendrils of energy slipped from his grasp and evaded him. He pursued first one, then another, and each would dart away, now existing and now wraithlike in its elusive disappearance. He began to sweat, feeling the muscles of his body sympathetically cording and knotting.

This wasn't the way. He was forgetting, interpreting the symbols his mind presented him too literally. What he was "seeing" there was no visual analog for, no direct comparison. But because he could not help visualizing in his mind's eye, he "saw" the snakes darting and weaving about him.

But they were not snakes. They were not solid tendrils to be grasped, twisted, broken and discarded. They were wisps of energy, ionization, ethereal and without substance.

16

He must come to grips with them as a *whole*, must repress and suppress them, to obliterate them.

He called up the last of his resources and created a great dampening blanket of force over them. A blanket which smothered and absorbed them, draining them away and damping them out, snuffing them as easily and dramatically as the flame of a candle.

It was anticlimactic. Once he had hit upon the right answer, the problem was solved, it was done. He went weak with relief. Then he found something else to his amazement: the energies he'd absorbed with his blanket—they had restrengthened him. *Of course! I absorbed those energies!* The blanket had been an extension of himself, an externalization which only faulty visualizing had allowed him to view as something apart from himself. It was fortunate, he realized ruefully, that so far his mistakes had been in his favor...

He looked up into the sky. There were no more crashes of lightning now; the freak display was spent. The thundercloud lumbered turgidly, overhead—empty of the *presence* which had energized it.

The enemy was gone. Whoever—*whatever*—that great power might be, at least he knew now he was not alone in the world, that perhaps the lot of even a Superman might not be an effortless one. He would have to guard himself even more closely, now. For his opponent had tested him, and found at least a measure of his strength, and next time—Max was sure there would be a next time, even if he had to initiate it himself—next time the going would not be easier.

As he gazed skyward, the first heavy drops of rain began to fall, splattering themselves with puffs in the dust at his feet, and pulling his attention downward again, back to life at hand.

Chapter 3

Fran stared at him with dark, anxious eyes. "Max—don't go."

The decision had been made. "It's the best way," he told her, standing with his hand on the door. "I'll act as though nothing's happened to me; pretend my defenses are down. It's that or just wait, you know. I'd rather be doing *something.*"

"There are other things besides driving a cab, you know."

"I know, Fran." He smiled indulgently. "But don't you see, if we just stick around here our thoughts are going to stay on that attack, and it will just sit there between us, all the time."

He palmed the doorknob, and carefully opened the door—the old way. "I'll be back from work this evening, Fran, just like always. Pretend it was all a bad dream."

She came close to him and put her arms up on his shoulders. "Take care, Max," she said. He bent and kissed her. Then the door to his apartment closed behind him, and he hurried down the stairs.

He was wearing a sport shirt and slacks, and he had his hack card with him. He'd phoned in; explained he'd been sick and felt better now and wanted the remaining half day's work. There had been no problem. That was one good thing about driving hack, he thought; you could pick your own hours, work your own time.

The heavy wood and glass door swung shut behind him, and he stepped, blinking, out into the hot sun on the bright stoop. There was a fresh, clean smell to the air; the thunderstorm had washed the grime from it for a little while. He trotted down the steps to the sidewalk and turned toward Central Park West. The sun was bright and hot on his back, and the air already steaming with water evaporating from the pools in the gutters and dips in the sidewalk. It was hard to realize, as he walked through the hot summer afternoon, that it *hadn't* all been a bad dream. To reassure himself, he let his vision change.

Waves danced before him, weaving a shifting curtain. Heat waves, he realized, from the sidewalk. Intermixed with them, different waves; water vapor rising back into the sky. And, lancing through them, the direct and almost palpable beams of the sun. Pure energy, those. He paused, fascinated. The wonder of it was all around him: the wonder of life, of substance—the miracle of reality. Wherever he chose to look, there were new marvels to behold. For a short spell he singled out a solitary dustmote and followed its crazy path as it rode the thermal currents—until suddenly his attention was broken as a man shouldered roughly by him.

"Goddamned crazy daydreamer," came the muttered oath from the other. Max stared after him, and then shook his head.

The wonders lay all about, and they were there for everyone, he realized; not merely those who held his extraordinary second sight. Perhaps they were less obvious for those who used only normal vision, but they were there.

When he'd been a small boy, Max suddenly remembered, he'd spent hours watching the minutiae of life crawl past him. He'd watched bugs crawling about their tasks, bees and butterflies in the flowers, clouds moving across the sky. The world had been full of new and strangely marvelous wonders for him then. He remembered hearing a far-off drone of sound and running out of his house to stare in delight as a tiny airplane flew over, high above. The world had been a brighter place then, it seemed. It was so much more full of primary colors, of life and movement. The world was a vastly bigger place then, the days far longer. And adventure lurked everywhere amongst the commonplace, no farther away than the nearest trail of ants, picking their way with uncanny precision to and fro along the same path that led to their ant hill.

He'd changed, Max thought. He'd "grown up." It was a process which seemed to occlude the brightness and clarity of one's vision, to dull the commonplace, and denude one's surroundings of their wonder. Was this what happened to everyone? Judging by the man who'd pushed so rudely past him, it seemed likely.

And yet he, Max, had been given a second chance, a second opportunity. He had been given a vision of terrifying clarity; one which stripped aside all those lifelong curtains of familiarity, and let him gaze again upon the world with fresh eyes.

It was a precious gift. It was a gift that could be easily misused—and one which brought with it the responsibility for *not* misusing it.

His thoughts turned toward the Other. Had that Other been given the same gift as he—but used it far differently? Or were there darker forces in this world which he was only discovering now—as they discovered him?

This gift had allowed him a new vision; stripped away the commonplace. What lurked behind the commonplace?

The thought was an uneasy one.

He'd been walking up Central Park West. To his right, across the street, lay Central Park. It chilled him to remember the place of menace it had become. And yet it amused him that while the park had a reputation as a place for muggings and juvenile delinquents, he had until this day always regarded it as a quiet, pleasant place to go when he had time free and wished peaceful surroundings. He'd never seen anything unusual happen in the park...until today.

Ahead, and to his left, was the great, brooding Museum of Natural History. It dominated its own small park, covering an area of several blocks. It was a gray and unlovely building, with its corner turrets and sooty stone, but he'd spent many rainy afternoons inside it; its collections seemed endless and he was sure he would never exhaust its wonders. There had always remained a bit of the wondering child in Max; it was a large part of his charm, although he was unaware of that.

As he drew abreast of the building, the sidewalk jogged to the left and stairs led down into the subway. He followed them down, his steps echoing emptily in the quiet afternoon air.

A passageway, cool after the sun that had beaten upon his back, led him to the coin booth, where he bought tokens. He went through the turnstiles and down the stairs to the lower, downtown, level.

The babble of the children met him before he came out onto the lower platform. Up ahead he could see them: a throng of perhaps thirty, ranging in age from eight to twelve, as near as he could guess. They were milling around with the usual aimless excitement of children on the loose and, temporarily, away from school. Several nervous-looking teachers rode herd on them, from time to time scolding them for approaching too near to the edge of the platform.

Several of the older boys were darting out to the edge, leaning out and peering down the tunnel, and then darting back into the crowd again, daring each other and taunting their teachers. Max walked down the platform toward them; the short trains they ran in the middle of the day would not stop at this end.

In order to pass the children, he had to skirt around them, following the open space near the platform edge. They laughted and joked among themseslves, and from the harried looks on the teachers' faces he knew none of them wanted to take another field-trip to the museum again. But they would, of course.

Down the tunnel there was a growing rumble, and, standing as close to the edge as he did, Max could see, down the tunnel beyond the station, the bright headlights of the approaching train. He hurried past the children to be free of them. Sharing a car with them was an experience he'd sooner avoid.

It happened just as he was almost past the largest cluster of them. He had turned to glance at them when suddenly one of the older boys jumped out of their midst, arms stiff, hands outstretched.

There was almost no warning—only the flicker of madness in the boy's eyes. Max felt the push and then he was falling, his arms pinwheeling, balance lost, over the edge of the platform.

For one sheer split second, he panicked. The lights of the train seemed directly upon him, and the thought ran through his head: *After all I've come through, to die like this?*

Then he reasserted himself. He braked time to a stop.

He was hanging motionless in space. There were no sounds. Time hung thick and heavy about him. Ahead of him, just entering the station, and suspended in what was almost full speed, was the train. The motorman was staring wide-eyed through the cab window, but could hardly have caught sight of him yet.

Carefully, his actions the cautious ones of a man who is attempting something new for the first time, Max shifted his position. Now, instead of holding a pitched headlong position, he was standing, still timelessly suspended in thin air, several feet above the tracks. Then, very carefully, feeling with his feet as though on thin ice, he began *walking* back onto solid footing.

Then he was back on the platform, and suddenly aware that he was still holding his breath. Sighing gustily, he released his grip on time.

And suddenly the.station was full of sound. There was the shrill screech of the train's brakes, the screams of the children and their teachers, and the shattering roar of the train entering the station. Max found himself feeling very weak and drained. It was an emotional exhaustion—the reaction of delayed physical shock.

He turned and studied the now-quieted group of children.

21

They'd seen him lose his balance and start to fall; they'd not yet adjusted to his steady presence safe upon the platform. He searched among them for the one whose eyes he knew—and found him. But there was no longer any madness lurking there; only a frightened child.

There was a pattern in the attacks upon him, Max realized. They all came in the guise of the familiar. Squirrels, pigeons, thunderstorms—and now a shove from a raucous boy on a subway platform. Had any of these attempts succeeded, his death would be assumed to be from freak, but "natural," causes.

It meant something else, too: he was under constant surveillance by the Other. He was glad he'd drawn the attacks away from Fran.

Yet—these attacks were childish. The Other must know by now that he could not be hurt by simply shoving him in front of a subway train. What was the point of it? To weary him? To keep him so alert that in his edginess he would make a slip of his own? It was impossible to guess the Other's motives or reasons... without knowing first who or what that Other was.

Well, that's why he was exposing himself, Max told himself ruefully. Perhaps in drawing the Other's fire he would discover his antagonist's identity.

For that was the hell of it: he was working blind. He'd had less than twelve hours to discover and master his own abilities—some of which, he was sure, he would discover only by trial and error. And in this deadly game of cat and mouse, errors couldn't be allowed. Max was sure he was his opponent's equal. His ability to fend off the attacks seemed to prove that. But tactically he was far from equal. He needed to know more—so much more. And he didn't know how to go about it. That was it, in the end: he was far stronger, now, but no wiser than he'd ever been. And he wondered about the Other....

At Columbus Circle, he got off the train and ascended again to the street.

He was at Eighth Avenue. Behind him was the tip of the Park, and surrounding the Circle were the Collosseum and the Huntington Hartford Museum. Down Eighth Avenue, the hurdy-gurdy of midtown Manhattan; neon lights flashing even in broad daylight, taxicabs honking raucously as they weaved in and out. A familiar sight, and one Max loved. He turned around. The huge weather sign across the Circle showed a temperature of 84. It was 3:30 in the afternoon. The sun, still operating on Eastern Standard

Time, shone down hard upon him from 2:30 in the sky.

Two and a half blocks down 58th Street, between Tenth and Eleventh Avenues, he walked down the ramp from the street into the garage of the Acme Club Company. After five minutes of banter with the dispatcher, he climbed into a Checker cab, slid his card into the clear plastic-windowed pocket where his name and face would be visible to backseat passengers, marked down the time on his schedule sheet, and pulled the car up the ramp and out onto the street.

The car was not one of the newer models—his penalty for coming in late—and the transmission balked when he pulled out onto Eleventh Avenue. For a moment he had the horrible feeling that he was being jinxed again, but his para-perception reassured him. Yet he would have to remain particularly alert now, for there were a thousand ways he could be gotten to, out here on the street in a car. It was very much like being the target in a shooting gallery, he thought. It was not a terribly reassuring thought.

There is an art to driving in New York City, and it was one Max had instinctively learned. Out-of-town drivers profess their fear of driving in this great city, but Max knew that driving was easier and safer for the skilled driver in Manhattan than in almost any other major city in the country. It was a matter of alertness, of being constantly aware of one's surroundings, the traffic conditions ahead, the timing of the lights, and most particularly one's fellow-drivers' habits. It was knowing when to go and when to stop. One did not play the game of Alphonse and Gaston with New York drivers; by the dipping of one's hood as one braked, as sure as the wave of a hand, one gave the other the go-ahead. On timed streets—and all the one-way avenues had timed lights—

one held the maxiumum speed, wishing only that the little old lady over there from Westchester would do the same instead of holding a steady fifteen and blocking traffic until inevitably the green lights ran ahead of her and the reds caught up.

Today Max found his usual alertness greatly aided by his new perceptive abilities. The aimless snarls seemed to be richly woven patterns, and he found he could sense them by the threads they dangled blocks behind, so that he could avoid them more easily.

Driving became a vast game, the city streets a checkered board.

Max felt a sense of exhilaration: the joy of playing a game and winning. It seemed absurdly easy to swing his way through the complex patterns of this dance of the streets. His car, now thoroughly understood and compensated for, responded perfectly to his unvoiced directions, and as he moved from fare to fare it was like a great square dance in which he changed partners with each new tune.

It was 5:30, the great homeward-bound rush was at its peak, and Max felt that at last he understood the challenge of life. He swung in to the curb to pick up a new fare.

The man was short and heavy. To Max's heightened senses, he was more than fat; he was gross. As the man wheezed into the seat and pulled the door shut, Max turned in his seat to look at him.

The man was well-dressed; despite the late afternoon heat, he wore a conservative black suit with a vest, and he looked unruffled. His face was round; what hair showed under the black homburg was neatly trimmed. He'd been recently shaved; talc still remained on his jowls. His expression was nearly expressionless; his face betrayed no emotion, and its lines were vague, indistinct.

But in Max's head a warning bell tolled ominously.

"Where to, mister?"

"Head uptown; I'll tell you where later," wheezed the reply. The man's voice was as thin as the rustle of long-fallen leaves.

As he pulled the cab out from the curb, a woman ran up to it and knocked on the window impatiently. Puzzled, Max gestured to his passenger in the back seat, and then noticed he hadn't dropped the flag on his meter yet; the woman must've thought the cab was empty.

Or—was it? He tried to *probe* the man sitting behind him. His original impression had been one of grossness. Now—he could sense *nothing*. It was as if the seat were indeed empty!

He flicked his eyes to the mirror; the blank gaze of the other met his. He lowered his eyes to the road again.

What new menace this—?

"You really have not the slightest chance, you know," wheezed the dry voice from the rear.

Max kept his eyes on the traffic ahead. "I've done all right so far," he said.

"Bah! We've only toyed with you. The game has only begun. How long do you think you can last?"

Max shrugged. "As long as need be, I guess." He paused. "Mind telling me something?"

The Other wheezed a vague sigh.

"Just what's your purpose? I mean, what am I to you?"

"Let us say you...upset the balance...."

They drove in silence for several minutes while Max thought to himself. Here he was, confronted at last by the Other: exactly what he'd hoped for earlier. But suddenly he wondered what good it had done him. The Other was an enigma; he knew little more now than he had before, except for—

"You said 'we.' Are there more of you?"

The Other wheezed again, taking his time replying. Max wondered if he intended to, and had about decided he wouldn't, when the wispy voice spoke again. "There are ten of Us. We own the world. I am telling you this so that you will understand—each of us has great powers; powers equal to or superior to your own. Against one of us—I will be, ahem, honest—I do not know. Against all of us—you have not one chance."

"So I pose a problem to you guys, huh?"

"You do. We have been in control for a long time, a very long time as you measure it. We—I seem to have made a small mistake; you were not supposed to reach maturity. It is a mistake I became aware of this morning. It is of course not to be tolerated."

"So what're you going to do about it?"

"I propose to you that you voluntarily renounce your Gift."

"Really? And why should I do that?"

"Because unless you do you shall not even remain able to enjoy your mortal life-span."

"You know something?" Max said suddenly after a moment's though, "I think you're lying. I think it's a bluff. You goofed, and you're in a spot now. I think it's a bluff. So you think you can frighten me back to where you want me. Well—I think we already argued the question this morning."

"Hmmmm," the Other wheezed, thoughtfully. "There are,

umm, more ways than one to skin a cat."

"What?" Max flicked his eyes to the mirror again. The back seat was empty.

He pulled in to the curb, stopped, and turned around to stare at the back of the car. He shook his head.

"Stuck me for the fare, too," he muttered.

Chapter 4

It was hours later when Max, weary and exhausted from the ordeal of the long day, returned home.

One didn't get something for nothing, he reflected grimly. Simply the effort of using his new senses and abilities had, added up over the long day, drained him. And he was ravenously hungry. But, more than that—why did every blessing turn out to be the opposite side of the coin of misfortune?

He pressed the buzzer for his apartment. Almost it seemed not worth it. What had he had, before this day? Not a great deal, in the material sense. But he'd had his own life to live as he chose, relatively free of interference, and it had been a good life...Fran....

Why hadn't she answered the buzzer? He pushed the button for her apartment. Maybe she'd returned to her own place.

Yet, when that...gross individual...had threatened him, it was as though he'd demanded Max give up his birthright. And—perhaps it was. It had seemed too precious then to surrender. But, what had he gotten himself into? He'd been alert and wary, the rest of the afternoon and evening, and all he had to show for it was his present exhaustion.

Where was Fran?

He started to reach for his keys, then shook his head angrily.

He stared through the gloom of the vestibule at the door. The gloom seemed to coalesce for a moment; then the door latch clicked, and tumbler fell quietly over. The door opened, and he walked through it, his measured steps almost like a sleepwalker's.

He trudged up the steps; levitating them would've required

greater effort.

He stopped first at Fran's apartment. It was empty.

And, when he got to it, so was his own.

"Fran...?" His voice hung in the air, the dying vibrations questing every corner of the small rooms. But there was no reply. There was no sign of Fran.

He had known, ever since he'd rung and received no answer. He hadn't wanted to know; he'd tried, ineffectually, to delay the knowledge that she was gone. Because this meant something new. Now he must finally face the question he had not wanted to face:

How much did Fran mean to him?

What *was* she to him? Was she more than a convenient prop for his ego? How much of his love for her was real—and how deep did it go?

Love is a word used freely in modern society. It is a word thrown about with abandon by the movies, the pop songs, the comic books—and by everyone, who wishes he too could be part of that culture. But what is love? Is it finding someone when you're insecure? Is it magical moments when the whole world turns technicolor and forty hidden violins croon from beyond the background? Is it sex, a moment of orgasmic release with another body? Where, in this confusing welter of symbols and experiences, lay love?

Who could tell? Love is a bandwagon. You hear about it when you enter adolescence, and an increasingly younger, earlier adolescence at that. Love is what Mary and Joe, they've been going steady for three weeks now, have. Love is what the man in the jukebox is moaning about, what the actors on the screen are mimicking. Love is what you don't have.

It colors your thoughts, inevitably. A starving man thinks only of food. But love is a word; not a tangible concept. It conjures up blurry images: the fellow with the pretty girl—you wish you had a pretty girl to show off that way—or that night when you stumbled on that couple in the dark; sex and love and romance are all jumbled and confused in your mind, and you only know it's something you don't have yet, that you want.

You seek it. You find yourself dating, too; only somehow she's just a pretty girl, and you don't feel on the inside what you try to show on the outside, as you do your best to impress the others with your success. You don't really communicate with her; you swap banalities, talk about school, sports, anything but what really preoccupies you.

Then, later—and perhaps not so much later, either—you're in

a dark room with her. It doesn't matter who she is, which "her" she might be; perhaps she's the girl your buddy boasts of having made, perhaps she's a girl you've been secretly infatuated with for half a year—or perhaps she's merely someone convenient and female. And, never so alone before in your life as you are with her now, you sweat and you grope, and you begin unraveling the mysteries of sex. And, after it's all over, you wonder if this can possibly be all it is. Your arms ache, from supporting your body, and somehow, although you gained physical release, your mind seemed always distracted by a thousand nagging details and questions. Is it safe? What if somebody should come in now? You kept slipping. She was bony in a surprising place; it was uncomfortable. You were nervous, anxious, awkward. And perhaps—just barely—you were sensitive enough to wonder: what is she feeling? Am I doing it right for her? But you don't know, because despite your fumblings, your kisses and caresses you really don't know her at all. *Is this love?*

Perhaps you thought that was love, but in the back of your mind you knew it wasn't. You felt obscurely ashamed the next time you saw her. You blushed, couldn't look in her eyes. You never really noticed *her* reactions.

What is love? Now you're older, more "experienced." You've gone through all the motions.

What is love, Max?

The jarring ring of the phone made him start.

He stared at it, and it continued to ring.

Dreading the message he knew was waiting for him, Max picked up the phone.

An unconsciously operating paranormal sense warned him. He did not put the receiver to his ear.

Snaking from the mouthpiece, a wispy tendril of greenish vapor darted back toward his hand.

It barely brushed him, but it stung. He dropped the handset and leaped back. The odor of decomposing matter lay heavily in the room.

The vapor branched, and sent questing fingers probing after him.

From the handset there issued a tinny boom of laughter.

He was weary; God, he was tired. Where was it going to end? Was this their plan? To wear him out, slowly and methodically, until he could not resist their attacks any longer?

He did what he had to do. The vapor writhed with almost visible pain, then it retreated, back into the phone. He let the handset lie where it had fallen, upon the old worn rug on the floor.

"Quest? Max Quest!" It was a tinny, wheezy voice. He knew it.

"Well?" he asked. He did not approach the phone.

"We have a young lady. I believe she, hmm, belongs to you."

There are more ways than one to skin a cat.

"Yes," Max said. His voice was dead.

"She is only mortal, and of very little concern to you now, I imagine," the voice wheezed. It had taken on an oily gloss now. "In your present state, you will not find it difficult to obtain others for your needs."

Max felt a raw ache within him. It was not true, he knew. He could not find other Frans. Nor had he thought of her in terms of his own needs. She had become a part of him. It was a sudden, galvanizing awareness. He had no longer been thinking of himself alone when he visualized his future. Unconsciously, he had included Fran. And now this Other—this wheezing, gross, and smugly satisfied voice that spoke hollowly to him from the receiver on the floor—awakened and underscored his understanding.

"What have you done with her?" The words sounded foolish to his own ears: the dialogue of a thousand melodramatic double features of many Saturday afternoons.

"Ahhh! You are vulnerable! Ahah!"

Max straightened. "You obviously had a purpose for this call, and I doubt it was the childish trick with the gas." His voice was firmer now.

"Ummm, yes. Quite so. Why don't we continue this conversation, umm, face to face? You'll find me in the law offices of Edwards & Archer." The voice gave an address in lower Manhattan's financial district.

"We shall be waiting for you," the Other said. Then there was an audible click, and the line was dead.

The night was ominous when he stepped out into it. It was cool and clammy; a fog had crept in from the river, and he could hear the distant forlorn calls of the foghorns.

But—this was the middle of the summer. Fog occurs when a warm air mass moves in over cool land—never in the summer. Now that he thought of it, Max realized he'd never seen fog here in New York City at this time of year before.

The Others...this must be their doing. Max felt tired and chilled.

As he headed for the subway station, he walked past the New York Historical Society building. It had a large and imposing edifice.

There was a sudden crash behind him, and he jumped, whirling. Fragments of stone bit angrily at his skin, and then he was sneezing from the thick dust.

There, smashed into the sidewalk not five feet from where he'd been when it fell, was a section of the building's cornice.

As he stood and contemplated it, a foghorn called mournfully.

They were herding him now.

The fog began to close in on him, masking nearby streetlights into glowing patches, muffling the sharp sound of his steps. It was cold and wet, a slimy sort of wet—wet with greasy overtones, like the harbor water with its filthy oil slick.

He was so damned *tired.*

It made him so angry; he knew they were goading him, forcing him to extend himself. And because he had to, he did it.

Slowly, the fog thinned, parted, withdrew. How far it had extended he did not know, but he had pushed it back a block in each direction.

He stumbled, and then leaned against a lamppost. He was shaking, and he caught himself.

Ahead, coming toward him, was a taxi; an empty, cruising taxi. He hailed it. The ride downtown would give him the opportunity to rest, for at least a short time.

"Where to, mister?" the cabby asked in a dry, dead voice.

Max gave the address without thinking, and the car pulled smoothly away from the curb.

It was so comfortable to lean back in the seat and relax; a cabby's holiday, almost. But he glanced at the windows with vague professional interest. How would the cabby go? Down Broadway?

The area beyond the windows was gray, an empty, fathomless void.

Max jerked forward in his seat. The view through the windshield was also gray. Not even the twin tunnels of the headlights showed through the thick fog...if fog was what it was.

"Hey," Max said, grabbing the driver's shoulder.

The man's shoulder crumbled in his hand.

He pulled his hand back, frightened now, and stared at what he held. Bits of cloth—dry and old, like a mummy's wrappings—and bits of...dirt?

The driver turned to look at him over his shoulder. The man's face was hollow and empty, his eyes vacant sockets.

Careful, warned an iron-hard segment of Max's mind. *Control yourself.* Control, for Max, had new, finer meanings, and with great effort, he brought himself under *control.*

First he must calm himself. He slowed the release of adrenalin into his bloodstream and lowered his metabolism to a more relaxed state. It would be no good to have his thinking clouded by panic now.

Then it was necessary that he perceive the reality of the situation. He opened his eyes anew.

The creature "driving" the car was a construct, a simulacrum. It had no life of its own, and never had. It was under control of the Others. But, under the circumstances, what could be gained by seizing it from them? He was on his way to meet them; would it not be wisest simply to relax again and let the thing deliver him to his destination?

But—*was* he being taken there? There was something palpably *wrong* about the way they were traveling. Worried, he used his paraperception to see beyond the blanket of gray that shrouded the windows.

Nothing. Nothing but unlimited space.

Where was he?

Desperately, Max wrenched at the door of the car and yanked it open.

A sudden howling gust of wind tore the door from his grip and wrenched it loose from the car. Max made a quick grab for the edges of the door frame, and, gripping them tightly, looked down....

Wisps of moonlit clouds floated by, and under. Through them and below them he could see the twinkling lights of the city. And with his other senses, he could feel the distant warmth and movement of the people in the city.

The car he was in was flying at great speed, high above the city.

For a long moment, Max clung to the door of the car, staring down. The wind whipped against him, tearing at his clothes. It was a thin, cold wind, and his hands were growing numb.

He shot a desperate glance at the car's driver.

The wind was cutting through the car now, and as it snapped and tugged against the creature in the front seat, it frayed and unraveled the thing's clothing. And, as the rotted cloth blew free, the creature's body seemed to disintegrate. It was blowing to pieces.

Yet the creature did nothing; it did not even seem aware of its plight. The interior of the car held no sound but the rising howl of the wind.

The lights of the city were starting to fall behind them, now, and below it was black and empty. They must be over the water, and Max suddenly wondered if this was a test he could survive. What did they mean to do with him? Dump him in the Atlantic?

Straining against his own fears, Max tensed himself, braced, and pushed himself through the door.

His hands did not want to release their grip: it required an act of will to unfold each finger from its iron clutch. But then he had done it—he was free. He gave a last kick against the car body, and threw himself out, into space.

The most important thing to remember was that he had time.

He had all the time in the world; all the time he needed.

His first reaction upon falling was sheer, paralyzing fear. His muscles locked with panic, and his brain raced like a car out of gear. But he had time. He had time to become aware of himself again, to slide out of his fear, and to discover within himself a vast wonderment.

He was plummeting down through the air. The wind ripped and tore at his clothing, nearly stripped his shirt from his back. It made his eyes stream with tears, tears which flowed back along the sides of his face as quickly as they appeared.

He tried to remember what he'd heard about skydivers, whose peculiar sport was to dive through the air for many long moments before opening their parachutes. They had learned to do acrobatics, to speed or slow their fall by spreading their limbs or holding themselves like a ball. He tried stretching his arms out, amazed at the pressure of the air against his flat palms. He stretched out, and it was almost as though he was swimming through some new half-liquid substance. He found that by inclining the planes of his hands, he could twist his body this way and that. It was almost like flying.

There was only one reason he'd taken the chance and jumped. He'd been able to levitate, back in the long-ago morning. In fact, his awareness of change was when he'd awakened to find himself floating over his bed.

He was not at all sure of the extent of his power to levitate. He had never thought of trying to fly with it. But, he thought wryly to himself, he would surely be finding out soon enough.

How long since he'd jumped from the car? He could not tell. Time, for him now, was completely subjective. If he wished, he could deliberately slow or suspend time, and spend an eternity caught high in the air. It would not be necessary, of course, but it

33

He gave a last kick against the car body and threw himself out into space.

did allow him the opportunity for trial and error in his levitation. He could halt time and his plunge, even feet from whatever might lie below—or simply by slowing time enormously, float down as slowly as a feather. But there would still be the tremendous inertia he'd generated in his fall. He could still splatter over whatever he hit, even if for him it all occurred in ultra-slow motion.

He could make out individual lights below. The angle of his fall and the prevailing winds had brought him over southern Brooklyn. Almost immediately below and to his left was the gracefully lighted arch of the Narrows Bridge to Staten Island. Immediately below him were the tree-shaded street-lights of residential Bay Ridge.

Carefully, he began to assert control over the magnetic loops of gravitational stress which banded the sky above and below him. He established, and then broke, restraining links with them as he fell, each contract acting to slow and retard his fall a little more. Until, finally....

Totally disheveled, he dropped to the sidewalk on Brooklyn's Fourth Avenue.

An unshaven old man stared at him, popeyed, and shook his head.

A dog barked with the sudden yelp of startled anger from somewhere behind him.

Max smoothed his hair with one hand while tugging his shirt and pants back into place with the other. Then he started walking, at a fast trot, toward the subway entrance on the next block.

As he headed down the stairs, he felt automatically into his pocket. His pockets were empty. He'd lost wallet and change while falling. He shrugged, then walked through the exit gates. There was no challenge from the token booth behind him.

Chapter 5

Max was prepared to find that the address he'd been given was phony. But when he found the building it was there, and the building directory said *Edwards & Archer, Attorneys at Law.* He signed the ledger held for him by a toothless old man and then took the automatic elevator to the fourteenth floor.

It occurred to him as he was riding up that it was not truly the fourteenth floor. He'd glanced idly at the floor buttons, and with distracted amusement he'd noticed the jump from 12 to 14. There was no thirteenth floor; the building was prey to a common modern-day superstition. Well, rather, there was no *numbered* thirteenth floor. For his destination was the thirteenth floor none the less.

Then the doors slid back, and he was facing a hall. The building was not too modern, although the bank of elevators was new; the floor here was marble, with a long carpet runner laid down along it. The entrances to different offices were ornate, their gilt spelling out in the standards of another day the respectability and financial responsibility of the people whose names appeared upon their doors.

His footsteps muffled in the carpet, Max followed the hall to the only door through which light could be seen. He paused for a moment before the door.

The hall was cold and empty; it was hard to imagine that during daytime hours it would be traveled by ordinary officeworkers. A faint chill spread through him. Perhaps it wasn't. What arcane business would Edwards & Archer conduct here in these offices, anyway?

He was still weary, but the fall through the air had swept the cobwebs from his brain and left him feeling exhilarated and newly prepared for the confrontation. And he'd met with no further obstacles on his way; while he'd maintained alertness, he'd also been able to gather his strength.

Pulling himself up, he reached out with his mind and pushed the door open. A shield of forced surrounded him with what he hoped was adequated protection as he stepped through the doorway.

It was not what he'd expected.

He was standing on a raised entranceway which extended before him a few feet, and then fell two steps into a great sunken room.

It was not an office; it was an open room of the sort one found pictured in the expensive men's magazines. The floor was covered with a thick-piled wine-purple carpet, upon which smaller accent rugs had been scattered. Around each of these brightly colored rugs were grouped pieces of modern but comfortably upholstered furniture: chairs, settees, and sofas. Nearby were low tables and floor lamps, each lamp creating an oasis of warm light for its island grouping.

The room was full of people. Nearly every chair or sitting place was occupied; others—mostly young women—sprawled upon the rugs. There was a gentle murmur of conversation, its eddies washing back up to him like gentle waves on a beach.

He was nonplussed. This was not at all what he had expected to find. Where, among all these people—and there must be over a hundred—would he find the fat man...or Fran?

As he stood at the door, a beautiful young woman approached him. She held a glass in each hand.

"Won't you have a drink and join us?" she asked, her voice a clear contralto.

Max accepted the drink automatically.

Holding the glass in his hand, without sampling from it, he looked the woman over. On the surface...she was in her early twenties, her long black hair falling straight to her shoulders, low bangs crossing her forehead, the total effect being to frame a face which Max could easily imagine on the movie screen. She had the looks and poise of a model or actress, as well, carrying her slender close-sheathed body with a supple grace so long-studied that it had become natural to her.

Inside....

Max was shocked. He fully expected another simulacrum. He expected this to be one of the girls the Other had mentioned on the phone: a soulless husk made for his—or their—physical

37

bidding.

She was not. As nearly as Max could tell, she was simply what she appeared to be: an attractive, healthy young woman totally possessed of her senses. He plumbed from her mind her name, Sally Remington, and her occupation, actress in TV commercials. There was no sign of domination by the Others....

"I beg your pardon?" he said, realizing that she had asked him something.

"I said, do you know the people here?"

"No, I don't. But...." he hesitated, wondering how to phrase it. "I was, ummm, under the impression that I was to see Mr. Edwards or Mr. Archer. I had no idea...."

"Oh, yes," she said, with a warm smile. "Mr. Archer is a producer. He likes to throw big parties for people...in the industry."

"Is he short and very fat, with a wheeze?"

"Nooo...no, Mr. Archer is rather heavy, but he's very tall." She laughed. "He looks like a real Texan—you know: all beef and on the hoof."

"Perhaps he's the one I want," Max said. He peeered out into the room, but the gloom and its size defected him. He could see no one answering Archer's description. The girl was looking, too.

"I don't see him," she said doubtfully. "But that's all right. He'll show up again." She took his hand in a gentle, but warm grasp. "Come on; I'll introduce you around."

He let her lead down the steps and out onto the main floor. The carpet felt very rich under his feet, and the beautiful girl beside him numbed his senses. He found himself taking a sip of his drink. It was a Manhattan, and normally he did not care for them, but he found himself enjoying it.

Careful, be very careful...came the inner warning. But he simply could not jibe the surroundings in which he found himself with any feeling of menace. There was no taint of the Others within the room or the people gathered here that he could find. It disturbed him by its absence. He had come here to meet his foes in a face-to-face challenge; instead he found himself at a strange but typical New York cocktail party. It made no sense, but he would have to ride along with it and see what happened.

"This is Mr. Smith," Sally was saying, introducing him to a handsome light-skinned Negro. "Melvin Smith. He's the poet and playwright, you know. He's had two one-act plays Off-Broadway."

Smith thrust forth his hand, and Max took it firmly.

"Weren't you a jazz magazine writer a few years ago, Mr.

Smith?" he asked.

The man's grip was soft and wet and lingering. But his tone was suddenly violent as he thrust his neck out and his head forward. "Yeah, man; I used to write for those ofay journals until, man, like I just couldn't stand the draft no more. Too much! You white cats parading us blacks around like you owned us, owned our music!" The smile never left his face.

Max drew back as though he'd been stung. "*Your* music?" he asked.

"Yeah, man, jazz is our music. You white cats had four, five centuries to goof it your way—you know, Stravinsky, Bartok, Stockhausen, them cats—but we got Bird, Bud, Monk, and Mingus. We got Ornette. And you know what you can do about that, baby? *Yeah*, that's what you can do about it!"

"I wasn't aware you played an instrument, Mr. Smith," Max said.

"Like, I blow the whole racial horn, white boy," Smith said.

"You're not doing badly at it, either," Max said.

Smith's smile grew wider, and then quite abruptly he turned his back on Max.

Max found Sally still at his side. "Is he always like that?" he asked her.

"It's a role he plays when he's in public," she said. "He's really a very nice man when you get to know him."

"Well, I guess it doesn't hurt his royalty checks," Max said dubiously.

She introduced him to a variety of people as they moved from group to group, and Max found himself wondering if he had stumbled into the prototypical gathering of show-business people. They were all here: the high-pressure boys, the career girls, the men who made the girls their career, the men whose taste found other, more "artistic" outlets, the classic jungle of the exploited and exploiters. As he moved from one to the next, Max began formulating the theory that these people were the only ones of their kind in existence; that all the others who populated the worlds of television, publishing, and advertising were simulacra created by Edwards & Archer, based upon these people.

"And what do *you* do, my dear boy?" asked a woman whose age would be underestimated by twenty years from any distance of over ten feet. Max was fascinated by the transparent top to her dress; she wore nothing under it.

"I drive a taxicab," he said, and waited for her reaction. He'd had two more drinks handed him in succession by the faithful Miss Remington, who remained at his elbow. But, aside from a bright cheerfulness he'd not known since late that morning, lying on the grass in the park, he felt no effect from the alcohol.

"A taxicab! How droll," laughed the woman. She gave Max a wicked glance. "Would you care to go to bed with me? As you can see, I'm really quite well preserved."

Max felt himself blushing furiously. Sally maneuvered him away from the older woman quite deftly, gentle laughter following their backs.

"Has Mr. Archer returned yet, have you noticed?" he asked Sally, wanting to find something to say before she commented upon his reaction to the proposition.

"I haven't noticed him yet, no," she answered. "Would you care to sit down?" She gestured to a nearby couch.

It was deceptively comfortable, and designed to hold only two people, so they had it all to themselves. Max sighed and set his empty glass on the end table to his left. Sally curled her feet up under her and let herself lean gently against him.

Nearby three well-dressed young men were chattering among themselves, accenting their conversation with occasional punctuation from their arms and hands, which swept in liquid gestures. Max averted his gaze from them and stared at the couple across from them, sitting on a sofa like their own.

The girl had folded herself against the young man, and the man seemed incongruous and out of place in these lush settings. His face was raw and looked sunburned, his hair an unruly mop. Unlike the well-dressed people around him, he was wearing a rumpled sportshirt and unpressed slacks and his shoes were scuffed and dusty.

Max stared at him for a long time before he was aware that the gaze was being returned, and longer yet before he perceived the truth. He was staring at his reflection.

The room was a large one, but, he realized suddenly, not nearly the size he'd thought. It was done with mirrors. Mirrors at each end of the room; mirrors which covered the entire wall seamlessly. He looked closer into the mirror, his brain suddenly clear. Yes, if you looked closely, you could pick out the opposite wall, too, where once again the image doubled back and retraced its path. The effect was one of an endlessly repeating infinity.

As his senses returned, he became aware of something else. He was no longer tired or hungry. He felt curiously refreshed. Piqued, he introspected...and discovered that his body had converted the calories released by the alcohol to body-building purposes. Once again he had reconverted energy for his own use.

The girl beside him seemed to have gone to sleep. Her hair brushed against his ear; her cheek rested on his shoulder. He wondered what time it was, and then discovered she was wearing a small watch. Its hands stood at midnight.

Suddenly he felt alerted. His senses screamed a warning.

He stared into the mirror again, his eyes searching the room behind him.

There were fewer people left now; the crowd had thinned by well over half. His eyes roved from group to group, and then....

Standing by themselves were two men he'd not seen here earlier. One was a tall, thick man who towered over everyone near him. His face was beefy and impassive. And with him...*it was the man!* The man who'd been in the taxi that afternoon, whose voice had spoken to him over the phone this evening. The man who'd threatened him: the Other.

Heedless of the girl at his side, Max came quickly to his feet and whirled.

Sally gave a soft cry and opened her eyes to stare at him with a startled look.

Max ignored her and stared disbelievingly at the room.

Far across it, his figure stared back at him. There was no sign of the two men he sought between them.

But...beyond....

Beyond his reflection, with their backs to him, were the tall man and the fat man.

He turned to stare again into the nearer mirror.

There, much closer now, the two men stood. They stared mockingly at him. Then the short, gross man lifted his hand and beckoned with his finger.

Without taking his eyes from them, Max quested with his paranormal senses.

The room behind him was empty of their evil presence. Just as it had been when he'd first entered.

But ahead of him, *beyond* the mirror, waited two Others.

Their presence smote his senses as though he had been simultaneously plunged into a bath of fire and ice. Quickly he throttled back on his sensory mechanisms. He felt dangerously close to a circuitory overload. And then he realized it had been *their* doing: a feedback amplified along his open and defenseless sensory paths.

The Other gestured again, beckoning him closer to the mirror.

Sally was standing now, and she grabbed his arm. "Max!

What are you doing?"

"Don't you see them there?" he asked, pointing at his two malignant hosts.

"See what? That's a mirror, silly. You've had too much to drink, I think. I'm feeling it myself. Why not—?"

He shook himself loose of her and advanced upon the mirror.

As the girl stared in speechless astonishment, Max extended his outstretched hand into and through the mirror.

It felt like passing your hand through a basin of water, he thought, and he fancied the surface of the mirror rippled faintly around his arm. But he could still see his hand, extending beyond the mirror, as though nothing was there at all. Resolutely, he followed it, and stepped through.

He found himself in a room exactly like the one he had left, but mirror-reversed. There was one significant difference, however. On this side of the mirror, only he and the two Others were real. Those reflected from the other room existed here as pale and insubstantial ghosts, although he could look back and see their solid selves in the room beyond. The ghost of Sally Remington stared unbelievingly into blank space, then, lips moving soundlessly, turned away. Max knew that he had disappeared from her sight.

The furniture, like the other inanimate furnishings of the room, was quite solid, however. And, Max's senses reported to him, the room and its contents were quite real.

"Welcome, Mr. Quest," said the shorter of the two Others. His voice held the same wheeze, but now, standing beside his partner, he did not seem to carry the same gravity of substance; there was something faintly apologetic and uncertain about him.

"You will remember me; I am Edwards. This," he wheezed, pointing at the Other beside him, "is Archer. Did you enjoy our little party?"

"Was it for my benefit?"

"Oh, my, no. Do you think we'd really go to that much trouble? You saw for yourself: they're quite real.

"To tell you the truth, we hadn't really expected to see you here at all."

Max allowed himself a grim smile. "Yes, I know." Then he nodded at the phantoms moving slowly and unseeingly about them. "What is their purpose?"

"Do they need one? An ulterior purpose, I mean?" Edwards asked. "We enjoy the company of real people, you know. Archer and I—all of us—we tire of manipulating puppets. It is much more pleasurable to move among the unknowing, the foolish *homo sapiens* out there, and take our pleasures of them, with their *cooperation.*" Edwards smiled, a smile which suddenly made Max want to smear his face into a featureless blob. Those people out there, with all their foolish vanities, were being exploited on a plane they did not know existed. Edwards and Archer, cloaked in the respectability of the roles they had chosen for themselves, toyed with and manipulated these people in the most subtle fashion: on their own terms. It was a refinement of control which had passed beyond their paranormal powers. They exploited the base qualities they found in the people themselves.

The Max remembered his original purpose here.

"Fran," he said. "What have you done with her?"

Edwards gestured across the room at a distant grouping of chairs and a sofa.

Heedlessly, Max strode past them and across the room.

The sofa had its back to him, and it was there he found her. She was lying, unconscious, stretched out upon the sofa. There was no mark upon her.

"Fran!" he said, stooping before her and touching her brow. It felt cool to his fingers, and, in growing fear and bewilderment, he picked up her hand and felt her wrist for a pulse.

It was there, but slow and almost imperceptible. Her metabolism seemed almost in suspension.

He rose. The two stood close by, staring at him without expression.

"What have you done to her?" he asked.

"I am afraid we have sent her to another place," Edwards replied.

"Sent her to another place. What do you mean?"

"You see before you a body; an, ummm, empty husk. The motivating force—what would you call it?—the, hah!, soul or thetan. It is gone. This is simply a body. A mechanical body. Reflexes, nothing else."

Max felt himself crushed, as though a great vise gripped his temples. "Her—soul? *What have you done with it?*"

"As I said," Edwards replied, unperturbed. "We have dispatched it elsewhere."

"Why? What do you hope to gain from this?" Max cried.

"Ahh...what, indeed? I will be frank with you, Max Quest. We wish to be rid of you. And there is but one way we can accomplish this. We must provide you with a motive. I admit we feared it would not be strong enough, but you seem to be quite strongly motivated; as well as we might wish.

"We have sent the thetan, the essence, of your Fran into

another dimensional reality. If you wish to regain her, you will have to pursue her there and find her."

"I see," Max said. "You cannot attack me directly, so you have used Fran."

"It is a symptom of your weakness," Edwards wheezed with a pitying tone of indulgence, "that your emotions are easily touched. Observe," he said, and pointed at a nearby phantom of someone from the room beyond. It was Sally. "She could easily be yours. She is real; she requires no domination from your vast powers. She singled you out and attached herself to you unbidden. She is real, and in your own terms, good, for all that she is only human...." He underscored his words with a sneer. "Is she any less than your beloved Fran? Or—any more?"

It was their last attack, Max realized. A most devious attack. Its purpose was not to destroy him physically, as their others had been—but rather to destroy him in a far more subtle fashion: to bring him down to their level, and make him one of them, ancient, jaded, and inhuman.

"How can I go after Fran?" Max asked.

Chapter 6

CHAPTER SIX

They tricked him!

In the blackness that washed over him, he could feel his strength draining way—and, with it, his new-found gifts.

He was spinning, spinning deep down into himself, as though in the center of his being there was a vortex that sucked him into himself and then threw him outward—he knew not where.

"Another dimensional reality," Edwards had told him.
Another reality. The phrase had meant little to him then; only a place, a destination in his quest for Fran.

Another reality...things would not be as he'd known them. Perhaps—but, would there even *be a* physical reality to correspond to or contrast with the one he'd known?

There was no way of knowing; he knew only this: In this new reality he was entering, he would be without his most powerful weapons. He would be defenseless, stripped of the powers he had suddenly inherited less than twenty-four hours earlier.

He awoke slowly, his temples throbbing in the heat. He opened his eyes, and lances of fiery light pierced them, striking a nerve which ran straight to his brain.

He groaned, and turned over.

His chest burned; it felt as though it had been rubbed raw. As he shifted, a sharp stone dug viciously into his bare hip. And his skin felt dry and sore, his muscles stiff.

The heat was on his shoulder and his back, now, and he opened his eyes again, thin slits this time.

Glare smote against them, but he kept them open. And

looked at his surroundings.

Yellow, sun-drenched stone was all he could see. A great plain of stone, sand, and clay that stretched to a far-distant horizon, where a cloudless and brazen orange sky cupped down to meet it.

It was hot, terribly hot, and as he licked his lips, his mouth felt dry and puffy, his lips cracked and swollen.

He pulled himself into a sitting position.

He was naked. The body was his own, as near as he could tell; he'd never had any scars or marks, but it *felt* like his own body to him.

It was a badly abused body, too. His chest, the front of his arms, his torso, the fronts of his legs, all were burned an angry red.

Carefully, he glanced up. A sun, smaller than he remembered it, but white against the orange sky, blazed down upon him from nearly overhead.

He wondered if he'd lain there all morning. It seemed likely. Nearby, behind him as he'd originally faced, was an upthrust cropping of rock. It cast a meager shade, but one he made for gratefully.

The ground was not smooth, although it looked deceptively so. His feet, tender and long-unused to barefoot walking, protested angrily the sharp creases in the rock, the scattering of pebbles, and the frying heat. When he slipped under the shelf of rock, he was limping.

He took stock of himself, then.

He was alone, naked and totally weaponless, on an alien world, in an inhospitable desert. He wondered what his chances were. Did people live in this world? Did anything?

The second question was more easily answered. Near where he squatted, a small thorny plant struggled up through a crack in the rock.

He looked at it carefully. The stems were blackish brown, the thorns from a half-inch to an inch and a half long and black. The leaves were short and close and silvery green. They reminded him of sage. He pulled a couple of the leaves from the plant and crushed them between his finger.

To his surprise, they were rather thick, and when he crushed them, a thin, greenish sap spread over his fingers. Cautiously, he lifted his hand and sniffed. There was no odor that he could detect. He stuck out his tongue and touched it gingerly to one finger.

A needle of fire shot up his tongue, and he jerked his hand

away hurriedly. His tongue touched against his inner cheek and the pain spread there. Hastily he rubbed the sap from his fingers in the loose dirt close by.

The pain subsided quickly, leaving him feeling numb and depressed. His mouth, now that it had been tantalized, felt dryer and more parched than ever. Would everything he found on this world be poison? he wondered.

Then another, bleaker, thought passed over him. If he found survival this difficult—what had Fran's chances been?

It has been a rigged trap, he realized. And he blundered directly into it.

But there was no real choice. It was this road or the other— the one which led to his rejection of his values and his principles, to his inevitably becoming one of the Others. He had sensed it that night, standing in the phantom room, surrounded by the shades of living people. His choice was simple: pursue his values, or give them up.

It was an attractive alternative they'd presented him. That trap he'd easily sensed. The girl, Sally: she was untouched by their evil, and in that lay their message. They had no need to contaminate their possessions if they chose not to. They could enslave without creating slaves. And they offered their world to him, too—a world which would corrupt him as easily and as surely as it had corrupted them. It would have been painless, and every step a pleasurable one, if his conscience could have been held in check.

But instead he had chosen to follow Fran, and his true obligations.

Despite the heat, he shivered. He'd followed the right path. What tortures of the body or spirit must Fran be undergoing in this world—if, indeed, she still lived?

God, he was thirsty.

The shadows that protected him from the sun's direct glare were lengthening now, and he wondered how long the days were here. That sun was a brighter, hotter sun than any he had known, and it would keep him pinned here until dusk. Another two or three hours out there lying in the sun, he knew, and he'd have been dehydrated and dead.

It was easy to laze here under the rock. The rock was dry and warm to his touch, but it was cooler than the rock beyond. The skin was badly burned all down his front, and now it felt curiously greasy and very sore. He'd had no food for a long time, either, and it was easier to forget that if he stayed quiet.

47

What existed beyond these dry plains, he wondered. Was the whole world a desert?

The sun had dropped enough now so that the glare was no longer upon the land. The sun was somewhere behind him, its rays striking the earth obliquely, reflecting off away from him. Heat waves still shimmered out there, making the distant horizon blurry and wavering, but he thought he glimpsed mountains.

Closer at hand, he could see the desert floor was not as featureless as he'd first supposed. Here and there were shelves of rock, not unlike the one he'd taken shelter under, thrusting themselves up at odd angles from the baked clay that surrounded them. There were also occasional cuts, dry washes he supposed, shallow and often petering out into nothing after short distances. The ground was not as flat as it had looked, either, and now that there were longer shadows, he could pick out hillocks and hummocks, and here and there vague scatterings of dense shrub brush. All of it had a silvery hue, and he wondered if anything but the poisonous thorny bush grew out here.

As the afternoon wore on, clouds appeared in the sky. First as scattered puffballs, then later gathering into massed but ragged banks. He watched them hungrily. Clouds might mean rain, and rain meant water.

When the sun had set down closer to the horizon—Max reckoned it at about five o'clock, although he had no way of knowing how long this world's hours might be—he rose and stretched. He did that unwillingly, for every movement strummed a chord on aching muscles. The shadow of his rock stretched long ahead of him, and to his right—he'd arbitrarily decided to apply compass points that followed the sun; that made it south—there was a darker, angrier cloud bank. As he watched, he saw what seemed a tiny spark arc down from it to an upthrust mesa, and then a column of dark rain descended upon that land.

It was many long miles away.

It came no near as he watched. A gentle breeze slowly picked up, and he found it to be easterly; it would blow the storm away.

The breeze felt good upon his skin, though, and he was at least grateful for that.

Now at last he walked around his rock and stared into the west.

The sun hung low above the horizon, its color shaded now to a fiery yellow, and its circumference bulging into a squat oval. It would be setting soon.

Max looked for sign of some relief from this endless desert, but saw none. He could not even glimpse the ragged sawtooth of mountains on that western horizon. And nearer the desert looked no different than it had to the east.

He would die out here, Max knew, if he did not find water, and find it soon.

He doubted he could last out another full day.

And food: so far he had seen no evidence of animal life. But nightfall was fast approaching, and Max remembered enough of desert lore from his own world to realize that most desert creatures ventured out of hiding only in the coolness of night.

Preditators big enough to search for him did not bother Max. He was concerned only with food of his own.

Wincing with each step, he began circling out from his base rock, searching for something, some sign of life. He watched most carefully when he crossed strips of dust, and then, realizing the futility of searching the hard clay and rock,and mindful of the easier going for his feet, he began following the dust.

Dust had collected in the hummocks and shallow dips, gathering into a dry stream which sought the lowest levels. It meandered here and there, sometimes spreading out across a broad area, sometimes narrowing to a trickle and even dying away. But Max kept to the dust, searching closely as he did, for sign...any sign: tracks of some sort.

The light was glowing redly across the desert when he found them.

They were a series of little scampering two-toed trails which crossed and crisscrossed the dust where it was fairly wide. Max judged that they dated over a number of days, and that thought depressed him again, for it reminded him that rain here would be scarce and seldom.

But he began following the tracks.

The tracks had a way of zigzagging back and forth over each other, but, taken into account as a whole, they followed a remarkably straight path. Max decided to follow them first back toward his rock and the north.

The dust ended shortly, but the tracks had pointed straight ahead, so he followed over bare rock and then cracked clay, and when he struck another dustbed he found the tracks again, still pointing straight ahead.

He followed them up and over a short rise, and then, by the dying light, he made out something he'd not noticed when passing this way earlier, to the west: a series of small black holes. There were perhaps half a dozen, scattered in no real order, over the hard clay of the hillock. The holes measured two inches across.

He'd tracked the creatures to their lair. The question remained, what lay at the other end of that path? Max hoped his guess was right.

He followed the tracks across the wide dustbed where he'd first picked them up, his own big prints incongruous alongside the neat little tracks he'd now become so familiar with.

Only once their path veered: to skirt another rock outcropping. Then they dipped down into a ravine, one bigger than any he'd encountered before.

He was certain of himself now, and the sight of a larger clump of shrubbery ahead clinched it for him. Max broke into a trot, and as the last rays of the sun disappeared, broke through the brush into the waterhole.

Unmindful of the possibility that his body chemistry might be too different from that of this world, he bent and plunged his head into the small pool of water.

At first he was content to feel the soothing touch of the water on his skin and to open his lips and let his mouth fill with water. He sat up and held the water in his mouth for many long moments before releasing and swallowing it.

It tasted good. Sweet and pure. He cupped his hands and drank his fill. Then, carefully, he let himself down into the pool and sprawled his full length in the water.

He'd not noticed it rising, but already a moon had come up over the horizon. It was large—larger than the moon he remembered by over half a diameter. And its light was nearly as bright—although far cooler—as the day's sunlight.

He stood up and examined his surroundings.

The pool was perhaps twelve feet across, and shallow. It was floored by a shelf of rock, which dipped at one end where the spring bubbled up from below. There was some sand, rimming the pool, and desert brush. There was no stream; the dry air and earth sucked up as much water as surfaced here.

The brush was not all of one sort. By the moonlight it was all the same silvery white, but the leaves varied among the different types and some had no thorns.

Max did not spend much time by the pool. By the moonlight, he could see many different tiny trails leading down to the water, and he was reminded of the trails he'd followed. Carefully, he stalked up along the ravine, and then hunkered down to wait.

He woke with a start. It was much darker than it had been, and high above the heavens were alight with a thousand pin-pricks of jeweled light. These were stars, and stars richer than

any Max had ever seen. He'd heard before that in the desert the air is clearer, and the stars brighter, but there had been no sights like this in the world he'd come from.

The constellations were all alien to him, but they dazzled with rich colors. He could pick out stars that were green, yellow, orange, red, even blue, a mixed bag of celestial plunder, rich for the plucking. For many long moments he was lost in the wonder of it.

Then he remembered why he was here, and he cursed himself for falling asleep.

He stood and stretched and looked around.

No sign of life or movement. The big moon was low and yellow on the western horizon. He turned back to the east, towards the waterhole.

A second moon was rising. This one was far smaller, its tiny crescent almost too short in diameter to be distinguishable. It was obviously at the beginning or the end of a phase; Max wished he knew more about such things. It shed scant light.

The desert was a different world, now; one without shadows.

Max moved down to the trail. He'd scuffed out the dust prints that had lain there before. He squatted now, and searched for fresh sign.

There was none.

It came to him then that he'd been stupid. He'd followed the trail closely for its entire length. His scent would lie along it. The little animals would not come tonight.

He cursed himself, but without conviction. At least he had found water. He was ahead by that much.

He thought about that some more. There could not be much water hereabouts. The little tracks had come a fair way to this spot.

And there had been other tracks leading down to the water.

Carefully, cautiously, Max began to make his way back toward the pool.

At first he thought there was nothing there. Then he realized that the light was deceiving. Across the pool, on a shelf he'd not touched, sat four small animals.

He was surprised by their very familiarity. They looked at first like prairie dogs. In his mind Max dubbed them desert pups. Their coats were light, of a shade near that of the rock. It was impossible to make out color. Their faces, paws, and short stubby tails were darker.

One of them was sprawled out on the rock, his forepaws dipping into the water. He appeared to be making washing movements with his paws, like a man soaping his hands, or—it suddenly came to Max—a raccoon washing his food.

As Max watched, the tiny creature lifted his paws out of the water and dropped something on the rock to one side of him. Then he picked up something from the other side and repeated the washing movements.

As he did this, one of the other creatures darted forward and snatched up whatever he'd washed, settling back on its haunches in a sitting position and bringing whatever it was to its mouth, like a squirrel with a nut.

Max watched, fascinated.

The little animals had brought with them to this pool a collection of what looked like nuts or seeds. They brought them in their paws, one at a time, in a straggling succession, while the washer continued his task of washing them carefully in the pool. After each pup had delivered his load, he would wait patiently in line for his turn to snatch up a freshly washed one and eat it. Once one became impatient; and darted forward out of turn. There was a great deal of angry chirping, and the transgressor was cuffed into the pool, from which it climbed wet and chastened. The animals were amazingly well organized, Max realized.

He was to the west of the creatures, and downwind, so he had not been discovered. Carefully, he gathered three good throwing rocks. Then, setting himself carefully, he drew his arm back and let fly.

The first rock smacked into the pile of unwashed seeds, scattering them among the suddenly chirping and scrambling animals. Disgusted and angry at himself for missing, Max fired again, without pause. His second rock hit one of the animals, almost by chance, for the creature had been leaping from where the first had struck and had dodged directly into the path of the second stone. The pup gave one shrill bleat and dropped. The others, keening shrilly, darted up the bank and away.

Max was sorry for them; they seemed an organized and industrious little band of animals. But in the desert one could not survive on sentiment. He needed food.

He was ravenously hungry when he reached the animal's shelf, and he picked up the limp body of the desert pup without thinking.

Then he paused. It was a furry animal, and he had no knife for skinning purposes. Nor the means to a fire. He scouted around, but the rock near at hand was crumbly clay or a heavy stone red with iron. There was nothing he could use for cutting.

As he held the animal in his hand, he felt it stir. It was not dead; he had only stunned it. Carefully, he clamped down on rising emotions, and then he dashed the animal's head against the rock.

His hands grew bloody as he used them to tear the skin away from the pup's small skull and then work it down off its body. The hide was tough and not easily torn. Several times he had to bite through it in order to separate it. The odor of the fur was dusty and musky, but not truly unpleasant.

Max ate the animal raw. The flesh was tough but not as tough as it would have been cooked, for the cooking process toughens before it tenderizes again. The animal's blood was salty, and its meat gamy in flavor. He found he'd finished it in remarkably short order. He washed his hands in the pool, and then took a drink of water.

The water had a vaguely bitter taste that he'd not noticed before, and for a moment it puzzled him. Then he shifted weight, and sat upon something small and squishy.

It was one of the seeds the animals had been washing. It was covered with a silvery fur, not unlike that which characterized the leaves of most of the plants nearby. It felt soft to the touch.

Holding it in his fingers, Max dipped it in the pool and washed it. As if by magic, the silver disappeared, and when he withdrew it, it was a pale color.

Curiously, cautiously, he sniffed it. There was a sharp odor, like that of a ripening fruit. He pinched it, and juice squeezed out. Remembering the thornbush leaves, but also remembering that the animals ate these fruit, he tasted the juice.

It was faintly acid to the taste, but sweet, not unlike a citrus fruit. He put the fruit in his mouth and bit it.

It was spongy in consistency, filled with little cells containing the juice; cells which broke and splattered their juice on the inside of his mouth as he chewed. The fruit made but one brief morsel; then there was nothing left but a few hard pit-like seeds, which he spat out.

Moving up the pool, he took another drink of water. Then he looked up.

The small crescent moon was high overhead, and the sky was lightening to the east. Day would soon be breaking.

Mindful that anything might help serve as a future tool or weapon. Max gathered up the bones and skin of the desert pup and found all the remaining desert berries, as he christened them, on the shelf. Then he rounded the pool to the east side, where the rim of the cut would give him some respite from the sun.

Soon he was asleep again.

CHAPTER SEVEN

In the days which followed, Max found himself toughening to the desert life. The first days were the hardest. His sunburn grew an angry red and kept him in constant itching agony until finally it began peeling. He spent much of his time in the water then, lying on his stomach and floating.

He lived on the desert berries and the desert pups. He fashioned snares from strips of their hide and placed these along their trails. At times he varied this by waiting in ambush with throwing stones.

He became proficient at stone throwing, practicing each day with targets. He made a breechclout and a pouch in which he carried selected throwing stones.

At first he used dried bones as crude knives, but as he scouted wider areas around the water hole he discovered one rock outcropping from which he could separate thin slivers of shale. Most of these were too brittle for sustained use, but among their layers he found an occasional layer of hard rock, and from one such he fashioned his first real knife.

He had done without fire. He had not needed it for his own comfort, for the desert held much of its heat through the night and dew settled faintly upon the rocks only in the hour before sunrise when already the sky to the east was growing light.

His feet were toughening, but at first opportunity he made a pair of crude sandals for them from animal skins. He had no way to cure the skins properly, but simply let them dry out and then pounded them with a rock until they were flexible again. The first sandals wore out quickly, but he made more, the new ones of double thickness and reinforced with the tough, fibrous leaves of one of the desert plants.

His skin became tanned and his muscles gained new tone as he lived these busy days and nights, sleeping the long mornings, working in the afternoons, hunting at night, and then returning to sleep again before the sun rose. And, gradually, he gained familiarity with the land and discovered the desert a far more hospitable place for life than he had first dreamed.

But toward the end of his second week, he was becoming worried.

He had been here long enough, now, to have gained some measure of pride in his accomplishments. Yet he was no great distance from where he has started. He had learned to survive, here in the desert, but he was no nearer to Fran than the day he arrived. Soon he would have to think about leaving this place. And a more immediate reason was the growing scarcity of the game.

The first week Max had found an easy time of it, preying upon the sturdy little animals who came from colonies in every direction to wash the poison from their fruit. But gradually these animals, despite the way he varied his modes and places of attack, had turned wary, and either he had severely depopulated them or they were finding other springs to drink and wash at. In either case, the situation could not continue as it was much longer.

It was on the ninth day that the wolves came.

There were six of them, and the first sign of them was when Max was scouting his traps and snares.

It was late dusk, and the desert was fiery red, the sky overhead blue-black, streaked with purples which shaded into bright reds as they approached the horizon. The sunsets were unbelievably beautiful here, Max had to admit. Indeed, the whole desert had a raw splendor that sometimes made him wish he could carve out a true homestead here and never leave it.

The snare was empty, but it hadn't been. The tracks in the dust he'd carefully brushed clean after setting the trap told the story. A larger animal, one with a three-toed paw, had raided the snare, killed and taken the furry prize.

Max sat back upon his heels. This was the first sign that anything bigger existed in the desert. He felt for his knife.

He was sitting at the pool, concealed in the shadows under a rim of rock, when they came down to drink. Five came to the water's edge and began eagerly lapping. But the sixth remained above, where it could command a view and mount guard.

Animals seemed to exist in well-trained groups on this world, Max observed to himself.

These animals were doglike, as big as collie dogs, and with short gray-striped fur. They reminded Max of nothing so much as wolves, and wolves they became in his mind from that moment.

As he watched them, he thought about them, wondering and worrying. Their presence here could only accelerate the depletion of game. They had already raided his traps and probably caused a meatless night for him. The subsistence level here was too meager to share with six wolves.

The wind shifted then, and his scent carried suddenly to the drinking animals.

The nearest raised his nose and sniffed, then growled. Immediately the other heads came up, and there was a shift in the pack's posture. The lead wolf came padding down the bank to join the others, and it seemed his eyes could pierce the deep shadow in which Max crouched.

The bigger moon shone fully upon the scene, etching it brightly in blacks and whites. Suddenly Max realized his own danger. He would make good game for these wolves; better than the little desert pups. Carefully he felt in his pouch for the throwing stones. They were small, weighted to be thrown accurately, and to kill or stun the small pups. Would they stop a wolf?

He could see the lead wolf tensing to lead the charge around the pool. It was time to act now, before they were set!

He jumped to his feet then, a stone in each fist, and began throwing the stones, quickly and with deadly aim—transferring a stone from left hand to right, throwing and fishing up a new stone with his left simultaneously. He had practiced, and he was very fast. The wolves were hit by a barrage of rocks and stones.

This was not at all what they'd expected; they were of the wild, and unused to anything but tooth and claw combat. When the first stone stung the lead wolf on the snout, it yelped and brushed a furious paw against its nose. When a stone caught another wolf in the ribs, that wolf turned and nipped at itself in vexation at its unseen assailant.

But the stones caused no real hurt to the wolves, and Max was growing desperate. He had to make them break into flight. He stooped and lifted a larger stone from the ground. It was too heavy and awkward to throw with one hand; he hefted it over his head with both.

The wolves had not broken formation; they were clustered in a dense pack across the pool from him. Max flung the stone with all his power into the center of that pack.

The night was split by a sudden scream of pain, and then the wolves broke. Yelping and snarling angrily, they darted for the brim of the cut and jumped up and over, to run off into the night, tails curled closely between their legs.

One wolf did not run. It was on its side, licking and chewing at its foreleg. Max found another large rock, and picked it up. This one he would have to kill.

Warily, not knowing how badly the wolf was injured, Max circled the pool. But when he approached the wolf, the beast did a curious thing.

It slunk down on its belly, rolling its eyes up at Max, and gave a strange, keening sort of whine. It's tail switched hesitantly from side to side.

Max, startled, looked closer. Then he saw it, faint in the moonlight, caught and half hidden in the thick fur of the wolf's neck: a collar.

The collar was a crude one, of woven thongs and looked old and frayed. But it betrayed the wolf's origins and it was the decisive factor in Max's decision.

It meant two mouths to feed, but it might quickly repay that effort; here was an ally, and—by extension—the most effective weapon he had yet found. He lowered the rock to the ground.

When he spoke to the beast, that seemed to reassure it, and its whimpering died to be replaced by a gentle panting and tail-thumping. Carefully, speaking steadily in a reassuring tone, Max dropped to his knees before the wolf and examined its leg.

The leg was broken. The animal let him examine it; indeed, it seemed grateful, whimpering only when he moved it in a way which must have hurt badly.

Using thin, flat bones, bones he'd once used as knives, and thongs from his pouch, Max fashioned a crude splint for the wolf's broken leg. Carefully he urged the animal to its feet, and found that it could walk now, with a pronounced limp.

He had been unconscious of it before, but now he became aware of a steady breeze at his back. It was stronger than the usual light breezes of the night, and it was from the west. And it carried with it a strange smell. He stood and looked about.

Dust and sand whipped by him in a sudden gust that funneled down the cut, and overhead he saw a great cloudbank moving swiftly out of the west. Its leading edges were already almost upon the larger moon, and edged now with a lacy silver belying the thickness of the bank which followed.

A storm! That was what he smelled. The strange smell of rain upon long parched earth, of lightning and ozone, blown ahead of the storm to presage its coming.

The wolf had its ears laid back now; it too sensed the storm to come.

A storm: what would this mean? Shelter, he'd have to find better shelter than was here. This cut—it might soon flood with the drainoff. He'd need a higher place—and yet one not high enough to attract lightning.

He could see the lightning, now, playing in the west. It seemed eerie to stand in bright moonlight, his skin caressed by the wind, and see to the west that great ominous area of black, lit by crashing bolts of lightning. The storm must yet be miles away, he realized; this was a vast desert.

Yet it was moving swiftly. Already the storm cloud's tendrils were above him, and then—the moon was gone, slipped behind the cloudbank, eclipsed by the storm.

It was darker now than it had been on any earlier night. There was a palpable, stygian blackness, and through it the wind still rose. The only illumination came from the still far-off flashes of lightening.

The wolf was crouching low to the ground again, his ears low, neck flattened. Max felt something cold and wet touch his foot, and in the next brief flash he saw it was the wolf's nose. Without thinking, he bent and stroked the animal's head.

Then, grasping the wolf's collar, he urged it to its feet again and made for the shallowest slope up the embankment.

Minutes later, the two stood on a low rise of land. Max strained his eyes to see westward for a hint of the storm's strength.

Then, suddenly, there was a white-bright flash of light, and the scene it momentarily revealed remained etched on his retinas in the thundering blackness that followed.

To the west, less than a quarter of a mile from where he stood, a great wave was washing toward him, sweeping across the rocky plains in a solid wall.

It had been impossible to tell: had that wave been only a few feet high, or—much higher?

The significance of the dustbeds was revealed to him now, as well as the barren, scrubbed look of the rock. Storms here unleashed great torrents of water which swept across the desert flats, washing them clean and leaving, after they were over, deposits of silt which dried into dust.

This rise offered no real safety. He would have to go higher.

The wolf sensed his feelings and gave an eager yelp as he raced it toward a nearby outcropping of rock.

The rock was like most of the others, a tilted shelf which slanted up into the air to a height of ten or twelve feet. Its angle made an overhang which Max would have chosen for shelter, had he not seen that advancing wall of water. Now, desperately, pushing the clawing, scrambling wolf before him, he climbed up the slope of rock for its peak.

There was another jagged flash of light, and by it he saw already perched upon the rock four of the furry little desert pups. They seemed numbed and transfixed by the dual horror of the approaching storm and the two newcomers. Max felt a great pity in his heart, but steeled himself to kill them, swinging a stone fixed in a thong which he carried as a slinging weapon. The wolf did not advance on the dead animals, giving fresh evidence of his earlier training. He waited for Max to gather them by their hind legs, hastily bind them with thongs, and sling them at his belt.

Suddenly the wind lashed against them, this time a colder wind that carried a hint of chill and the spray of rain. And below Max heard the sudden roar of the water.

He stared down into the impenetrable night, trying to imagine how high the water would come, hoping desperately that they would not be trapped between frying pan and fire and lightning would not choose their perch to strike.

The water slapped angrily against the stone, and sudden spray shot up and drenched them. Then the wavefront had passed on, sweeping on out, over the vast dessert. Max wondered what kind of storm could create such a flood of water.

He did not have long to wonder, for now from the west he heard another sound, the muffled roar of the rain. When lightning flashed again, he saw, incredibly close, what looked like a solid curtain of water, stretching high into the black sky, and for a moment he thought it was a second, far higher, wave. Then it struck.

Max threw himself upon the wolf. The wolf gave a startled snarl, then seemed to recognize his purpose. The two lay flat and huddled on the narrow ledge atop the rock. They could hardly assume any other position; the rain smashed down on them in a great torrent, beating them against the stone with great unceasing hydraulic hammers.

Max found himself laboring to breathe. Water flowed over his body in a constant stream, and he could not only feel but *hear* it drumming upon his back. He lay face down, sharing the open hollow beneath their bodies with the wolf; had his face been exposed to the direct blast of the rain, he knew he would have drowned.

It was cold, too. The temperature had dropped well over twenty degrees, he estimated, and the wind still howled out of the west, whipping the rain against his side as well as his back, drenching him with what felt almost like ice water. Max shivered, wet, gasping, and exhausted.

The lightning had progressed farther east, Max noted gratefully. He had worried about their high, exposed position here.

Then, after he had reconciled himself to a never-ending onslaught from the storm, the winds died and the rain grew gentler. Max wondered how long he had lain there, the storm smashing against him. One hour? Two? But it was dying now. The rain fell more like normal rain. His muscles aching, he struggled to a sitting position.

The rain fell off quickly after that, until suddenly, through a break in the cloud layer, he glimpsed a bright shaft of moonlight angling towards them from the west. While the storm had moved eastward, the moon had followed its own course to the west.

When the moon shone full and bright upon them, Max looked down upon a changed land.

Below was an area of vast lakes, of inland seas. The moonlight glinted off water far to the west. There would be no getting down from their rocky perch this night. Below, water still swirled and eddied in hidden currents.

Far to the east, now, there were still arcs and sparks of light. It was truly a vast and frightening storm.

Max untied two of the small beasts he'd killed earlier and gave one to the wolf. And, as the moon passed slowly farther west, he and the wolf shared a cold, wet meal.

They slept together until the sun rose. When Max felt its early heat upon his shoulder blades he awoke, startled for a moment not to find himself in the shelter of shade. Then he looked around.

The sun in the east cut down through a thick haze. But its light was still sharp enough to catch the desert in rare splendor.

The lakes he'd glimpsed by moonlight were smaller now, and the area immediately below was clear and drying. But amazingly, all along the edges of each of these many rain-pools had sprung up a vast profusion of plants!

As Max watched, still more struggled up out of the ground, their growth easily visible to his eye. And the earlier plants, having reached a growth of two to six feet from the ground, were proceeding to flower.

The flowers ran a riot of color, concentrating upon violent electric blues and scarlet reds. But all of the other colors of the spectrum were there as well. Max gazed down upon them, fascinated.

Then there was a stirring at his side, and the wolf was awake.

"Well, old man," Max said, his voice sounding strange and startling to his own ears in this strange morning, "we've survived." The wolf looked up at him with wide eyes, tongue lolling. His coat was still wet, and in the sun it steamed.

"You know, you tell me a lot," Max mused. "You've got a collar, for one thing; for another, you are obviously trained. That makes a pretty blunt suggestion for the existence of other men on this world...men who once owned you. But where do they live, eh?" The animal pricked up its ears at the question. "And what were you doing running with that wild wolf-pack?"

Max stood and stretched. His muscles ached, but he felt fit and ready for the new day.

Then he clambered down off the rock, the wolf following.

The animal showed no inclination to leave his side. Suddenly remembering what had brought them together the night before, he dropped to the ground and checked the animal's splints. The thongs, hastily fastened the night before, had worked loose and shifted about some after they'd become soaked in the storm, but now they were drying tighter. Max shifted them and checked to be sure they would not cut into the wolf's leg. The animal watched him in his ministrations with quiet trust and confidence, and once again Max was struck by the strange and well-trained loyalty of the beast. Whose pet had he been, and what had happened? He wondered if he would ever know.

They spent the forenoon in the shelter of the rock they'd slept on, for the sun's heat was no less vicious for all the haze. Indeed, the humidity only magnified the heat.

Max watched in wonderment the accelerated growth and death of the desert plants. These lacked the silvery sheen of the more hardy plants, and they had a fleshy insubstantiality to them. Occasionally a breeze would drift to Max from one of the clusters of plants, and he would smell the rich, heady fragrance of the flowers. Their pollen must be airborne, he decided. He'd seen few insects here in the desert, far too few to cope with this invasion of plantlife.

As the sun rose high overhead, the pools of water steamed

and shrank, new plants darting up along each new exposed strip of waterline. And, as these new plants began their life-cycle, those farther out were ending theirs. Their flowers shrank into seed pods, and as the sun struck their stems and leaves more directly, they shriveled and browned in the heat, the liquids of their life-sap sucked from them by the sun's boiling rays.

It was a whole life-cycle Max watched, taking place before his eyes in a few short hours, the seeds of these plants falling, hard and tiny, into the dust where they would remain until the next rainfall, to again sprout into a short-lived jungle. Somehow, it all seemed rather futile.

Chapter 8

The pools were much smaller, and most of the sudden desert plants dead, when they set out that evening on the beginning of their journey.

The wolf and the storm had decided the matter for him. It would not have been easy, even with the wolf hunting for him—if indeed it could be trained to do so—to find enough game to remain there longer, even if the storm had not hit.But the storm did, and it washed away sign of game trails as well as flooding out the underground chambers in which the desert pups lived. Their habit patterns would be altered too greatly now to make hunting them possible.

Max had accomplished much during his initial sojourn here in the desert. He had learned to survive in an outwardly hostile environment, equipped with only his brain and his naked body. But little good would have been served by remaining, even had game remained plentiful. He would only have been marking time, waiting for a break in routine to force the same decision.

He chose to head east, for only in that direction was the horizon interrupted by mountains. He had no way of knowing how far the desert stretched beyond the horizon in the other directions, but there at least was something concrete: a goal to strive for. He could only hope that something other than desert existed beyond that wall of mountains, and that he could find passage through them.

He waited until the worst heat was gone from the sky, then threw one of the remaining dead pups to the wolf and ate the other. It was not a pleasant meal, despite his present familiarity with the raw flesh of the little animals. The others he had eaten fresh-killed.

He had armed himself with a pouch full of throwing stones and the stone-and-thong sling. He had spent the afternoon practicing with it, for his encounter with the desert pups the night before had taught him that he was still too awkward with it. Not only was it suitable for use as a club, as he had used it then, but—and more to his original thinking—he could swing it around his head and then let fly with it with amazing accuracy and a killing speed.

Aside from these weapons, he had only his stone knife. He made a strange figure, he knew, clad only in the briefest furs, husky and tanned, the wolf trotting at his side. And yet there was about him the feeling of confidence, of having pitted himself against elemental odds and survived.

They had to skirt an occasional pool of water, but they made good time across the flats. They walked steadily and unceasingly through unchanging desert for many hours, the larger moon rising now before them, picking out their way. They stopped for a short time beside one pool, bathing themselves and drinking, and then they went on.

They had covered a good distance. Max estimated, when the sky ahead began growing lighter, the depth of it fading into pale blue over the mountains. The mountains looked a little higher, a little closer. He could pick out some details now.

They slept that day under a familiar outcropping of rock, but Max was worried. These shelves of rock had grown less frequent during the last few miles, and he saw few ahead. He estimated at least one more day upon the desert before they reached the foothills, and he wondered what they would do for shelter that day.

That afternoon they rose again, found a small remaining pool of water nearby, drank from it, and began scouting game. They found none. Worried, Max decided to push ahead, hoping to cross a game run on their journey.

That night went slower. They found a water hole soon after the larger moon had set and the smaller one risen, and tracks around it, but no sign of the desert pups themselves. They had come upon the hole too late; the small creatures were often about in the early evening, Max had found. Instead, Max had to content himself with a few of the desert berries. The wolf would not eat them.

Dawn found them still trudging wearily across the desert. There was no shade or shelter in sight. There were not even any sizable cuts or ravines here, the lips of which might offer some meager shade.

The sun in their eyes, they pushed on.

The wolf whimpered, his tongue hanging mournfully.

"Yes, old son," Max said in a tired voice, "I know—you're hot, you're tired, and you're hungry. So are we all, fella, so are we all...."

Ahead the land dipped a little, and as he crested the short rise he saw the familiar silvery-green of desert bushes. Achingly, he hurried down into the hollow, to the water hole there.

Both he and the wolf drank lingeringly there, the water helping to cool their bodies and slake their thirst. And, if one could not find food for one's belly, water was better than nothing....

Sitting by the poolside, Max rested his arm on a flat stone. When he put his weight upon it, it shifted slightly. Curious, he climbed to his feet and then stooped and overturned the rock.

The underside was damp and clammy, and, as he stared in astonishment, little grublike things began slowly and awkwardly to move for fresh cover.

With a short growl, the wolf was upon them, and in short order his tongue had swept them all from the rock shelf. He sniffed about, over the stone Max had overturned, and seemed disappointed there were no more.

Max was startled, but then, the idea upon him, he began searching for more stones he could overturn. He found several, and in each case found the pale, white grubs beneath them.

After the wolf had enjoyed what Max judged to be a fair meal of the grubs, he cautioned the animal, "Leave these next to me. I could use some meat in my diet, myself."

Fighting a rising emotion of repugnance, signaled also by the rising of his bile, Max grabbed a handful of the soft grubs from under the next rock. He paused, then dipped his hand in the water and washed them. Then, hurrying to overcome his own reluctance, he pushed them into his mouth.

They were almost tasteless, vaguely sweet, and very tender. Had he been served them in a stew, he realized he would not have thought twice about them. Except for the flavor, they reminded him of raw oysters.

Max and the wolf loafed by the water hole that day, Max taking frequent dips in the shallow water to combat the heat. Having overcome his revulsion against the grubs, he made a good meal of them that evening, before they started out again.

The terrain was changing.

At first it seemed that the way was simply growing more difficult; the ground was becoming more broken, giving way occasionally to loose boulders and sharper dips. It was stonier, too, and Max found himself wondering how much longer his crude sandals would survive the wear.

Then they entered the cacti.

These were the first cacti Max had seen, and from a scattered few they grew into a veritable forest, so many that it was impossible to hold a straight path between them for any amount of time.

The ground actually consisted of a raw form of soil, Max discovered. It was a sandy kind of loam, but the raw shelves of rock and broad beds of cracked clay had disappeared behind them. And where this new, gravelly soil existed, the cactus plants grew.

Most were single tall barrels, crowned at the top with thorns. But some had smooth sides, while others had spleens, and these edged with sharp thorns. Max was careful not to brush too closely against the thorny cacti; they looked as though they could rip his skin open as casually as a can opener.

When the eastern horizon lightened again, the mountains stood tall and sharp against the paling blue. They were close, now; less than a day away.

While none of the occasional scatterings of boulders stood tall enough to supply any real shade in the coming day, Max found one perched close over the shallow cut, and the combination sufficed him. With the wolf close at hand, he stretched out and fell quickly asleep.

He woke to hear the wolf growling softly. Max opened his eyes and stared.

The wolf was crouched at his feet. And, opposite his head, across the draw, Max saw a strange and almost unbelievable creature.

It looked like a huge toad. It appeared to be three feet across, and it was covered with fine scales. As Max stared, the thing looked directly back at him, blinking twice. Then its mouth gaped open, and a long forked tongue flicked out once. The thing hissed, and Max wondered: was this a carnivore, or did it exist on small insects alone? Was it going to attack? Was the hiss a warning?

The thing sat, implacable, waiting.

Max glanced up. The sun was dropping into the west. It was late afternoon.

The movement of his head alerted the thing, and he saw it tense.

Warily, Max leapt to his feet and to one side.

And as he did so, the toad-thing sprang into the air, landing were he had just been.

The next moment was confusion. With a doglike bark, the wolf leapt straight for the toad-creature, and, snarling, attacked it.

Max saw then what he had not seen before: the thin fangs on each side of the toad's wide mouth. Hissing, it tried to turn and sink its fangs into the wolf. But the wolf, betraying his familiarity with such an attack, had sunk his own teeth into the toad's hind-quarters and whipped himself out of range of the toad's fangs.

While the wolf worried and tore at the thing, Max seized his sling-stone and began swinging it, watching for a chance to let it fly.

The wolf was ripping and tearing the desert toad's left hind leg, and now, suddenly, the leg itself pulled loose. The toad, hissing venomously, turned; but the wolf, his mouth still gripping the bleeding leg, backed warily, growling.

Then the toad turned again, facing Max.

That was the chance he'd been waiting for. Max released the thong, and the whirling stone flew straight at the toad's head.

The crude missile smashed into the toad's skull, and the ungainly creature dropped. It was dead.

Max approached it with caution, though, and marveled at its size when he did. Its body was short and squat, measuring about three feet in length. But the leg that the wolf was now ripping and chewing had been at least six feet long. And the toad had given evidence of being able to hop a fair distance.

Using his knife, Max hacked away a hunk of meat from the other rear leg and bit into it. But the flesh had a strange taste to it and was very stringy. The more he chewed, the less pleasant it tasted. He finished the piece he had cut, but he took no more.

Instead, he began examining the creature more closely.

It was related in type far more to the gila monster of his own world than to earthly toads or frogs, he found. Its skin had a reptilian scaliness, its neck sheathed with concentric circles of tough armor plate. He pried the mouth open and found that the jaw dropped until the whole head could serve as an orifice. There was no doubt in his mind now that the creature would have eaten him if it could, swallowing and ingesting him whole, as a snake will a large victim.

The fangs were, as he suspected, ducted and hollow. He

The toad thing sprang into the air, landing where he had just been.

could not be sure whether it was venom or saliva which dripped from them now, but he was careful not to touch it.

After he'd finished his examination, he took his knife and began hacking at the joint of the other rear leg. Soon he had it cut loose, and then he attacked the creature's belly, cutting the skin and flesh loose in strips. The meat he rolled into compact bundles and then wrapped with the skin.

The skin on the creature's back was far tougher, and he had another use in mind for it. Carefully, tediously, he worked at it with his never-sharp knife until he had large ragged sections which he used, doubled, to wrap round the soles of his sandals. The sandals had not fared well and were now nearly in tatters. But this new scaly hide was far tougher, and with luck would last over the mountains. Max saved the remainder of it for future use, and used some of the strips from the underbelly to make bindings for it, so that the whole pack, including the extra meat, could be slung over his back.

Finally, his fascination overcoming his caution he returned to the fangs. They were a good six inches long, and he wanted them. They were thin and sharp-pointed, and he could think of many uses for them. But they would also make trophies. Hacking again with his blunted knife, and wrestling them with his hands, he cut them free of the beast's jaws, and let them hang, dripping, until he felt they were free of venom.

By now the sun was yellow on the horizon, and the wolf had finished its meal, leaving only the long slender bones of the leg he had torn loose. Max was tempted to take those bones, too, for they would make good clubs and might even be sharpened into spears, but his load was large enough, and he had another set stowed away on his back, still encased in their leg.

They set out again, still directly east, for Max saw a dip in the mountains ahead and hoped it signified a usable pass.

He had been walking for over an hour when thirst overwhelmed him. His mouth still held the unpleasant taste of the toad's flesh, and it came to him that he had not had any water for a very long time.

Yet there was no water to be seen. This was a different territory and he had no doubt that if one could dig, as the cacti had with their roots, one could find water, but none surfaced.

He toyed with that idea for a while, his thirst growing stronger and stronger. The cactus plants...they were great barrels, and undoubtedly their roots tapped underground moisture. Might they not be tapped in turn for water? It was done in his world, Max reflected. And, at this point, no other opportunity seemed to offer itself.

His choice seemed clear: there were two kinds of cacti predominating, the smooth and the spiny. The smooth-skinned cactus would be far easier.

He chose one of about his own height and pulled out his knife. But before he used it, another thought struck him, and instead he took out one of the toad's fangs. He could not be sure it was long enough, but it seemed worth a try.

The fang was a little shorter than his hand and ended in a root, which he had cut and wrenched away from the parent jaw. In the root end was a cavity, and the cavity dipped in to form a tube which ran the length of the fang, narrowing as the fang did, but exiting just short of the point, to one side. The fang seemed clean, but Max scrubbed it with sand, while the wolf sat on its haunches and looked on inquiringly.

Then Max took the fang and drove the point into the fleshy side of the cactus.

He was rewarded by an immediate trickle of clear liquid, and when he pushed the fang in deeper, the trickle increased to a steady flowing stream. He let it run for a short while, so that any remaining venom might be washed free. The water splashed upon the ground, where it sank instantly into the dry sand, and the wolf came and sniffed it but did not attempt to lap at any of the stream. Max was to remember that later.

Now, pleased with his success and luck, his instinct for caution satisfied, he put his mouth to the falling stream and drank.

The water had a faintly alkaline taste, but only a trace of it. It washed the lingering taste of the toad from his mouth and slaked his driving thirst, and Max drank long and heavy from the cactus.

Finally he was quenched, and he wrenched the fang from the cactus. Almost instantly, the spongy flesh of the plant closed around the hole, leaving only the scar of broken skin to mark the spot.

Max stood again, and, body heavy with the water, turned to continue along their path.

As he walked, the rhythm of his walking became alive to him, and he felt strangely heady. It was as though he was a finely oiled piece of machinery, thumping purposefully upon the dry earth. He paused, startled at this observation, and the cessation sounded inside his brain like the sudden shock of silence in a foundry.

What was wrong with him? Max stared around himself at

the great forest of cacti, and then at the ferretlike beast at his heels. The wolf slunk back from him, frightened.

Overhead the stars winked at him, blinking on and off. He stared at them, lowering himself to the ground, so that he could see better. His joints seemed afire, and the pressure on his knees as he knelt was that of a great weight. Without removing the pack from his back, he lay down upon the ground and watched the sky rock and reel overhead.

He knew one clear moment of sanity, before his thoughts disintegrated: *That stuff I drank—that wasn't water!*

Chapter 9

He was standing in a great room.

Tall mirrors stood unsupported at odd angles, their distribution being, as near as he could tell, quite random—and yet, no matter how obliquely he faced them, his own image would appear before him.

The lighting was low, the room as a whole illuminated only by a scattering of winking colored lights, set in the low ceiling. There was a touch at his elbow.

"Welcome, Mr. Quest. Won't you have a drink?" The girl was tall, cool, and beautiful, long dark hair falling in a cascade to her invitingly bare white shoulders. A twist of lemon peel kept the hair from her eyes.

"A—drink? Yes, I'd like that," he said. "I'd like that very much."

"Right this way," she said, taking his hand in hers and leading him straight for a mirror.

"Look out!" he cried, but she slipped easily through it and beyond. She looked back at him and beckoned to him.

She was only a reflection now, and there, beyond her in an animated group of people, he saw another familiar figure: short, pert, feminine. But her back was to him. "Fran?" he called, and then, hesitantly, he stepped into the mirror.

It smashed into a thousand pieces, falling in tinkling shards upon the floor with the sound of a waterfall splashing upon the rocks.

He found the girl kneeling on the rocks beyond, cupping one hand in the tinkling water. Her hair had fallen free and fell down around her neck and across her shoulder; it was not long enough to reach her small, bare, and beautifully formed breasts. Sunlight glinted from her hair with golden tones.

He stared down at the pool, then slowly raised his eyes past her kneeling figure, to the giant cactus perched above, the water falling from its side in an obscene stream. "No!" he shouted. "No! I won't touch that stuff!"

As he watched, the water took on a yellow hue, and the cactus became a huge man.

"Archer!" he screamed. "Archer, say something, just once!"

"He grew bored with speech three centuries ago," said a wheezing, bubbling voice beside him. Max turned and found Edwards. He reached down and seized the fat man by the lapels and tried to shake him, but Edwards was immobile, and Max felt himself blushing with shame and foolishness.

"A drink, perhaps?" Edwards said with a vaguely pitying tone, and handed him a glass.

Max accepted the glass gratefully, and then turned to look about him at the others. Somewhere...was she here? The desert plain was thronging with people, sitting, standing, talking; the clink of glasses blending with the breeze-like murmur of their conversation.

Nearby stood a group of three men and four women. One of the women was short and had short dark hair. Her back was to him. Still carrying his glass, he crossed the thick carpet toward their pool of light. It was cast by a floor lamp cunningly shaped like a thin crescent moon.

When he approached them, he was disappointed to discover that two of the women were only reflections in a nearby mirror. The remaining two were tall and had long blonde hair. Both they and the men with them were dressed in fine evening clothes, and the women carried light fur pieces dangling over their arms. Their voices rose and fell in sophisticated tones.

He stood close by them for a moment, wishing he could understand them, then raised his glass and started to sip his drink.

It tasted faintly alkaline. Shuddering, he cast it from him, the glass bouncing on the rug and then hitting a stone and shattering.

They turned and stared at him with polite surprise on their faces. Then one of the women began to laugh. The other joined her, and he looked down at himself and saw that he was naked. Embarrassed, he turned his back on them, but that only seemed to refuel their glee.

The girl was standing nearby. She shrugged out of her white garment and handed it to him. "Here," she said softly, "wrap yourself in this. It will do for now." He accepted it gratefully, not pausing to wonder at her own nudity. She was beautiful, but in an inanimate fashion, like a lovely statue.

"You're here to serve your forty days, aren't you?" she asked.

"No," he answered, puzzled by the question. "I'm looking for a girl."

"Will I do?" She moved closer to him and put her arms around his neck. The garment he had been holding to himself dropped away, and he felt the full length of her body against his.

"No, no," he stammered trying to get away. But her arms were entwined around his neck and shoulders now, her hands in his hair.

"Won't I do?" She moved her body against him, a rhythmical movement. Then she pulled his head down and pressed her lips against his.

Through the corners of his eyes. Max glimpsed the short dark figure he sought. Her back was to him. But she was starting to turn....

She mustn't see me like this, he thought, and broke free of the girl.

A wind rose, blowing him back, back away from the figure he knew was Fran, back toward the girl close by.

Then it was a stronger wind, and it had blown everyone away—everyone but Max and the girl. Did she have dark hair, or blonde? he wondered distantly. She was facing him, her mouth open, calling something out to him. But the wind whipped the words from her mouth and away from him. As he watched, horrified, he saw the wind catch in her mouth and distend it, drawing her lips back over her teeth, catching in her cheeks and puffing them out.

Shouting soundlessly, for he could hear nothing over the rising howl of the wind, he grabbed her.

A chunk of her bare white shoulder broke away in his hand, and then—as though he had plucked the loose end of a tapestry and it had begun to unravel—he watched her body fly to pieces, the wind eroding her into nothingness. Then at last he stood alone on the great empty plain.

"Is it love you want, or just my gratitude?"

He whirled at the sound of her voice.

"Fran!"

"Well, Max, I see you've found me."

"Ummm, yes." He felt nonplussed.

"Aren't you glad you found me, Max?"

"Yes. Yes, I am. Aren't *you,* Fran?"

"God knows I tried hard enough, but I just couldn't get away from you for long enough."

"What? *What are you saying, Fran?*"

"Do you think I *wanted* you chasing me, Max?" she asked. Her smile hinted at another expression; a leer, he thought.

"My dear," wheezed a voice. "Is this pest still about?" Edwards came from behind her, his head no taller than hers. He took her arm.

"Brush him off for me, will you, hon?" she said.

"Fran!" cried Max.

"Quest," said the fat man, "be missing."

"But, Fran! It was you—I did it for you," Max sobbed.

"No, it wasn't," she said, looking back at him over her shoulder. "You did it for yourself. What do you want now, a medal?"

A dark shape nudged against his ankle, and the wolf snarled.

"Fran?" Max called.

The wolf lunged, snarling, after her disappearing figure.

"*Max!*" she screamed.

He awoke, sweating, under the stars. There was no moon in sight. The wolf was crouched nearby, a low growling sound coming from its throat.

He felt limp and exhausted, as though he had been engaged in a long and grueling combat. His muscles felt strained and aching. His throat burned raw.

He struggled to a sitting position and shrugged the pack from his back. Unfastening it, he loosened one of the packets of meat and gave it to the wolf. The animal leapt upon it greedily and began chewing and tearing at the meat.

Max felt terribly thirsty.

Then he remembered. The cactus; the alkaline taste. He should have heeded the wolf's warning. It had not been water.

There were stories of cacti in his own world, cacti which secreted certain alkaloids which could cause sickness or hallucinations; some Indians used them, he knew, in their religious rituals.

This stuff had brought dreams, visions. He tried to remember them. But he could not. He could only remember that they were terrible dreams, and that they left behind them a lingering doubt, a distrust in his mission and in himself.

And the damned stuff left him as thirsty as he'd been before drinking it.

Carefully, he climbed to his feet. He felt weak, tottering. He needed water and food badly. Staggering, he approached another cactus.

This one was spiny. There had been nothing wrong with his logic; these plants did store moisture. Would his luck be better this time? With his knife, he scraped bare a portion of the cactus's skin. Then he forced in the fang again. This time it was not as easy; the cactus was less fleshy, and it was more like forcing it into soft wood.

But when he'd driven the fang in almost to its root, fluid began to flow from it also.

This time he did not sample it immediately. Instead he called the wolf.

"Here, boy; come on old man. Try this stuff, huh? Wash your dinner down."

The wolf, having finished its meal, trotted inquiringly over and sniffed at the wet ground. Then, extending its tongue, it began lapping the falling water.

Max waited until the wolf was finished, and then drank from the falling stream himself. It tasted warm and brackish, but like real water. He drank for a long time.

The road curved gently from the south.

He had been following a direct course toward the gap in the mountains when he encountered the road. It was evening, and he and the wolf had been walking since five o'clock, as he reckoned the sun's position; for two or three hours, anyway. Dusk was again on the land, and at first he thought his eyes were playing tricks on him when he climbed the rise and saw the wide ribbon of the road ahead.

It curved up from the south, following a northeasterly course which crossed his own at this point, curved again, and then straightened to point directly east for the gap.

It was a strange and marvelous road. When Max approached it, he found its surface worn and pitted in places, sand drifted across it where it dipped. It was old, so old and long-unused that no travelers' tracks betrayed themselves on the drifted sand, and a cactus pillar grew from one sand patch in the center of the roadway. It was wide; as wide, Max estimated, as a six- or eight-lane highway.

He kicked away the dust and sand and tried to guess at the road's composition. He knelt and touched it. It was black; that he'd seen from a distance: a black scar that cut cleanly across the tumbled land. Now he could look closer and see that whatever this black substance, it was more like stone than asphalt—it was a black obsidian, solid and without discernible seams. After he had followed it for a way, he found a place where a culvert had filled with silt, and a new waterway had eroded under the road there. He stared thoughtfully at the cross-section the break revealed. The road was over two feet thick here, and the break was clean, almost glassily sharp. The road makers might have poured a substance which hardened into a glasslike stone.

The road pointed now directly toward the mountain gap, and was already beginning a slow climb. Gratefully, he followed it. Even with the occasional breaks and drifted-over spots, the going was far easier than it had been through the surrounding rough country. He wondered how long he had followed parallel to the road before discovering it.

He wondered, too, about the road's implications. For it was a sign, and only the second he had encountered, that this world might be inhabited by intelligent beings. The wolf's collar was the first, and it told him little. But this road, now—! It told him much. It told him of a great, continent-spanning civilization, a nation of road-builders, who built, he was sure, for fast, wheeled transport. The road was well graded, slicing through low hills, following embankments over cuts and small valleys, and its approach up the mountain was gentle and certain. For the first time, Max gave thought to the possibility that the gap ahead was not a natural one.

But if the road told him of its makers' glory, it also told him of their downfall, for it was a road long-abandoned. No one had need of it now. No one but Max.

Imminent dawn found them high in the mountains, and Max was shivering. He had not stopped before now only because it was too cold to stop moving. He had paused, twice, to give meat to the wolf and to take small pieces for himself. He chewed on them, but with little appetite. The meat tasted unpleasant to him; it still carried the foul smell of that desert toad. And he had found since his strange seizure from the cactus-water that he needed little food, but was always thirsty. Fortunately, he had passed several mountain streams and been able to drink his fill at them.

He did not stop to find a place to sleep until the sun had mounted high in the sky. The air was thin here, and a long time warming. He lungs still heaved, minutes after he had lain himself down on the smooth roadbed, for once in no hurry to find shade.

He awoke late in the afternoon, feeling greatly refreshed. The sun was low and yellow on the great desert, and he stared back along his route, amazed at the great distance he had come.

He was high in the gap; perhaps another two hours would see him to its summit. As he looked back, he could see the road, its curves all gentle, leading back down through the mountains and then stretching out onto the arrid plain. He could see the distant curve where it started south, and then, a long way farther, where it curved west again. But high as he was, he could not see anything beyond the desert to the west.

He was a little sorry he had not headed south first; the road could not have been many miles south of his original hunting grounds. It would have made the way far easier going for him, perhaps shaved a day or more from his journey. But that was all of the past, done with. He had acted as he thought best at the time, and he could find no fault in his reasoning.

When he crested the gap, the sun was low at his back, and this side of the mountain range was in deep shadow. Far to the east he thought he could glimpse the glint of water, but closer the land was already deep in twilight and he could distinguish nothing.

It was cooler on the eastern side of the mountains; he strode swiftly, both to put many miles behind them and to keep himself warm. As night fell, so did the temperature.

The going was all downhill, and Max found it curiously tiring, more so than had been the climb. His muscles were not built for coasting, he decided.

The road dipped into narrow valleys and then climbed lower ranges, dropping steadily as it did so, but now providing a more varied pace for him. He had not imagined the mountain range to be this broad. He was still in the mountains when morning came again. They were low enough that the sun's white heat was quickly warming, however, and this time Max did not sleep in the sun.

He awoke earlier than usual that afternoon; the sun was still some distance above the range behind him. He was just as glad, he decided; night fell earlier here, and he had a great curiosity about the land before him. Somehow he sensed it would not be a continuation of the desert.

A mile's hike brought them to the crest of the last low range, this range more of a foothill to the mountains proper. Max stood at the brow of the hill, his feet planted firmly on the black road's roughened surface, and took in the panorama before him.

It was a land of fields and forests, of plains and hills. In the distance he could see two rivers which joined to the south. It was a green and beautiful land, and he felt as though he had come upon the promised land after a long sojourn in the wilderness.

The black ribbon of the road unwound itself before him,

stretching down and out, turning northward now, northeasterly, for the nearer of the two rivers. And, there on the near bank of the river, where the black thread ran to meet it—was that a city? Max strained his eyes, but the sun was already too low for good seeing. He would have to wait until he was closer.

Yet he was excited as he started down that last gentle slope. A city—people! At last he might come upon a land in which he could obtain decent clothing and food for himself,, and perhaps—his heart rose while his brain applied the ice-water of caution—perhaps, he might find word of Fran!

And yet...it would not pay to be too optimistic. The city might have suffered the same fate as the road. It too might be a long-abandoned artifact of a now-perished civilization. Yet it was a fertile land, and Max was sure he would find people in it. The wolf's ears had pricked up, and he held his nose high, sniffing, as he padded eagerly along the road. Max was sure the animal had come from this land, perhaps along this very road.

They ate well that night; the wolf twice darted off the road and into the underbrush which was now thick along the roadside to return each time with furry animals not unlike short-eared rabbits. Max took the first one, and ate it all. The second the wolf devoured. Max was surprised at his pleasure in the taste of the still-warm raw flesh; he had developed a taste for raw meat.

He called a halt long before dawn. It was warmer down here, warm enough that he would not suffer any great discomfort in stopping to sleep now. He wanted to come upon that city by daylight; a nocturnal life made less sense in this more hospitable land.

He slept that night in a soft hollow of grass, and to his hardened body it felt like a softly sprung mattress.

Chapter 10

The wolf was gone when he awoke. The sun was still in the east. It was around ten o'clock. He climbed to his feet and stretched. He felt greatly refreshed.

There was a rustle in the underbrush, and the wolf emerged, another rabbit-creature in its mouth. It dropped the dead animal at Max's feet and disappeared again.

After the two had breakfasted, and Max had washed and drank at a nearby mountain stream, they descended onto the plains.

This was a very different country from that they'd left behind. The land rolled, gently, and was luxuriantly foliated. Great trees grew alongside the road, hiding from view now that vast vista he had seen from the last ridgeback. Some of the trees dipped low across the road, arching until their limbs joined overhead, making a great leafy tunnel, green spotted with the gold of sunlight. It was a remarkably beautiful countryside, Max reflected, like that he'd known in his own world but for the small white sun. But here, under the trees, he did not have to think of that one difference, and instead he let himself feel a great peacefulness and one-ness with this quiet, beautiful world. To walk this road, now, was perhaps the most pleasant thing he could think of.

Gradually the trees thinned, and drew back from the road, and he was in a meadowland, dotted here and there with copses of trees and brush. And, ahead....

The towers of the city were broken, its streets choked with rubble and ruins. It was a city long dead. Trees grew in the open courtyards bounded by the remnants of once-tall walls and cluttered with the debris of long-collapsed roofs. Grass grew in the pockets of dust and weathered rubble in the still-indestructible streets; vines resembling ivy climbed many of the half-standing walls, coating them with a soft and leafy green, hiding their ugly scars. Yes, it was a city long dead.

Max walked its silent streets and stared in wonder. The streets had been wide, once, and were still passable in most places. Many of the fallen walls showed black glassy ruptures, although most wore lighter colors on their surfaces. Here and there Max found the red rust of what had once been metal...and that gave him some idea of the many years the city had lain here unattended.

He tried to find some hint for the cause of the city's collapse, but there was no sign of any uniform catastrophe. Some of the ruins still showed signs of fire-blackening, while others did not. Some buildings still stood tall among others which showed now only their ragged foundations. Earthquake, fire, war? In the end Max could only conclude that this was simply a city which had been abandoned, abandoned to the multiple ravages of time, all of which had done their work, singly and together.

He followed a northeasterly course through the city, staying on the road which had let him into it. Beyond there would be the river, and perhaps beyond that—? Max wondered. There must still be people somewhere; the wolf's collar bore mute testimony to their existence. Only—where?

One part of the city had withstood the passage of time better than the rest. This was the part along the river's edge.

Here the buildings still stood. They were not the towers he had found to the southwest, but low, long buildings, set upon terraces and served by curving streets. Max left the main road to comb one side street.

The street was narrower, and Max had to keep to the center, for the bushes and creepers had narrowed it still further. Many of the plants bore flowers, and Max wondered if they had once been part of the gardens which now overflowed the terraces. This had all the appearances of a once-prized residential part of the city.

He climbed, the wolf still close by, darting here and there to sniff at what Max assumed were animal runs, until he had reached the level of one of the terraces.

From here he could look down on the lower-lying parts of the city and see the still-clear pattern of the streets. There was a squared grid, and over it had been superimposed another, at a forty-five degree angle. Where both grids intersected there were circles and what must once have been parks.

In the other direction...The nearby river sparkled clearly in the sunlight. It was a broad, quiet river. Not far downstream it was joined by the other river; the city was located a little above their juncture. The land between the rivers was low-lying, and rich with verdant greens. And—was that a drift of smoke, rising from beyond that woods? Max strained his eyes, but could not be sure. The air here was thicker and hazier than it had been in the desert. Max suspected the desert had also been higher. It has struck him as he descended from the mountains that the way down had been longer by a good deal than the way up.

Max turned to look at the house on the terrace. It was two-storied, and gave the appearance of being split-leveled. Its sides were thickly covered with ivy and creepers, but the roof was still intact.

The door was wide and low, the doorway sunken in the thick stone of the walls. This stone did not appear artificial, either; there were closely fitted blocks which, as near as he could tell, held no mortar in their joints. Yet the joints were tight enough so that none of the plants crawling upon the wall's surface had found entry through them.

Inside, all was a shambles. Dead leaves filled the corners of rooms, and some showed evidence of being long unused nests.

There was wood here, but fortunately used only for what must have been ornamental purposes, for it was rotted and decayed. Max leaned against a doorjamb, and it disintegrated into a fine yellow dust which made him sneeze.

The house smelled musty, and Max wondered what he could find here, but he poked through its rooms none the less.

The rooms were far from bare, but their contents had not withstood time well; they were now littered with what could only be called junk. Max felt obscurely cheated.

But only until he found the kitchen. For there he found his first usable tool.

It was lying upon a plastic countertop, and when he picked it up it resembled nothing more than a cigarette lighter. It was small, flat, measuring two inches by six. The top, made of the same still-bright alloy as the rest, flipped back to reveal a thin coil and a pushbutton trigger. He pushed the trigger.

A thin beam of flame shot out of the coil.

He almost dropped it, but as soon as his finger slipped from the button the flame disappeared.

Cautiously, he tested it again. The flame winked on again, jutting out to a distance of about six inches. Carefully, Max relaxed his touch on the button a little. The flame lowered to two inches, then an inch. Then it died when he pulled his finger back.

What was it? A cigarette lighter in fact? It would be impossible to guess. But it was exciting to realize that at last he had again the means to a fire, and could cook his food. He flipped the top shut and hefted the gadget curiously. It seemed amazing that this thing alone, of all the house's contents, could resist the ravages of time. It was a solid-feeling thing. He tucked it into his pouch thoughtfully.

There might be other artifacts here. He began a closer search.

In a drawer, he found the knives. They were kitchen knives, made of some alloy as bright as the lighter he'd found. Their handles were of a plastic of some sort. He eyed them greedily. This was a treasure trove! But in the end he selected only two, which he judged the sharpest, and stowed them in the pack on his back. With the long bones of the second toad leg that he still carried, he now felt well armed.

The growl of the wolf in the doorway alerted him.

He stood well back within its shadow, waiting, listening.

He heard nothing. But the wolf was slinking carefully out, sliding along a low outer wall with his belly almost to the ground.

Suddenly the air held the sound of a heavy *twang!* and a long shaft smashed into the wall directly behind the wolf.

The wolf gave one commanding bark, and then leapt.

Max slipped to the edge of the doorway, knife in hand, and vaulted out, and up over the retaining wall onto the upper terrace.

The wolf was struggling with a man! He held the man's arm with his teeth and was pulling him down, forcing the man to his knees.

The man had dropped his weapon and was fighting bare-handed against the wolf when Max hurdled the wolf and put the point of his knife to the man's chest.

"Hold!" he said, and as he did so Max felt the wolf releasing its grip on the man.

He was hardly a man, Max could see now. He was a boy, a boy whose cheeks still held pale unshaven fuzz. He was tall and thin and awkward-looking, his skin pale, and his hair an almost white blonde. His face, contorted now in a combination of startled fear and pain, was thin and sensitive-looking, his eyes a pale blue-gray, his nose long and straight.

The boy was clothed in a simple tunic and pants, both of them bright-colored cloth, the shirt red and the pants blue, and both embroidered with fancy curlicues along the seams and hems.

84

At his feet lay an instrument which resembled a crossbow, and at his waist the youth had strapped a quiver of shafts for the bow, shafts like the one which had nearly hit the wolf. Had it hit him, Max was sure, it would have killed the animal. There was a great deal of power in that weapon.

Max flicked his gaze at the youth's arm. The boy was holding it, rubbing and nursing it, with his other hand. It bore only the red marks of the wolf's teeth; the animal had held him without breaking his skin. Again Max was amazed at the animal's training. Someone had trained him well indeed.

They held the static tableu for a long moment while Max took in his captive and his weapon, and the boy in turn studied Max with covert eyes.

Then Max straightened and kicked the crossbow away from the boy. "Now, what in hell am I going to do with you?" Max said aloud.

"Please, sir—I did not know he was yours," the boy said. He pointed at the still-alert wolf.

Max felt his mouth gaping, and closed it again. The boy spoke English! Or...did he?

His mind cast back, across the long grueling days, to that black moment that had presaged his presence here. He had known everything then, before his powers were completely stripped from him.

Another reality. However much this place might appear to correspond to his own, home reality, it was not the same. He remembered that he'd not been sure there would be any physical analogs for him here. But there were...if he remembered that he too was now a part of this reality, seeing, experiencing it from the inside, as a product of it.

The clue lay in the bodies. Max had left his body behind, on Earth, lying next to Fran's. Yet he had a body here, and it felt no different than it ever had, except for the toughening he had given it since his arrival. And Fran—she must have a body here as well. And if it did not resemble her other body, he might search for all his life and never find her. Very well; these were new bodies, like the old and yet unlike. For if this physical reality were in truth distorted, different from that from which they came, so were their bodies, in corresponding ways and indeed even their psyches, or thetans, as Edwards had called them. As a part of this reality, a subjective part, Max viewed and felt and experienced it as a world no different in the main from his own. But it was sufficiently different that his vast paranormal powers could not function here. And that was difference enough.

His body, though: it was a product of this reality, of this world. And without being aware of it until now, he now spoke in the language of this world as well.

"You—who are you?" he asked. His voice was deeper, more commanding than he'd expected.

"I, I am Ishtarn, son of Ishmight," the boy quavered, his eyes fixed now upon the bright knife still gleaming in Max's hand and still pointed at his chest. Max's near-naked bronzed and muscled body held him in fearful awe, Max could see. He smiled a trifle as he realized what a barbarian figure he cut, clad only in uncured and ragged furs, wearing a crude and makeshift pack of scaly hide. Yet, as the boy had uttered his father's name, he had seemed to regain some inner courage.

"Very well, Ishtarn," Max said, sheathing his knife once more in the pack. He picked up the crossbow and hefted it in his hands. "You fired upon my wolf, and my wolf disarmed you. You are unharmed; relax. Tell me about your father, your people. Where do you come from? Where do you live?"

The boy seemed more at ease now; he had realized his life was no longer in danger, and he recognized in Max a potential friend or ally.

He gestured across the river. "We are nomads, sir. We live in the lowlands. We herd animals. My father," his voice gained pride, "is the chieftain. He is Ishmight the Mighty, and...." His voice trailed off as he realized that he was boasting. "Who are you?" he asked with a child's naive directness.

Max smiled. People; he had finally met people. At last he was accomplishing something. "I'm Max Quest," he said. "I came down that road." He pointed to the southwest, to the black road.

The boy's eyes widened. "You came on the road, sir? But it leads only to—"

"The desert. Yes," Max agreed, "I came from the desert."

"I did not know it was possible for men to live in the desert," Ishtarn said.

"They don't, as far as I know," Max said. "I'm the only one—and I didn't stay there."

The boy gazed up at him with real awe.

The boy had crossed the river in a boat the resembled a flat-bottomed canoe to explore the dead city.

"This is the City Shanathor," he told Max, "and great legends are told of its passing. We of the plains are descended from the people of this city."

"What happened?" Max asked. "What destroyed the city?"

"Is it said that the people became too proud," the boy said. "And that their pride brought down the wrath of the firmaments upon them. I do not know; only, the legends say that there were great plagues and famines and other things beyond our imaginings, and all but a handful of people were killed."

"There must've been a world-wide civilization here at one time," Max mused. "I wonder if there were other survivors, in other cities...?"

"I do not know," Ishtarn said. "There are only the tribes of the plains that we know of. There is a story of a land far to the east, across the way of the great snows, and the City Paraganat, but no one has ever been there, and it may be only a story. I do not think there is another city in the whole world, for where would it be? The plains are empty, except for Rassanala and his raiders' fortress."

"The world's a big place," Max said gently. "You've never even seen the desert, and neither of us knows what lies beyond it."

"What is the desert like, sir?" the boy asked.

Max found himself sitting in the sun, describing the desert and its baked flats, the strange creatures and plants which lived upon it, and the terrible storms. Then the sight of his shadow, long on the ground before him, he reminded him of the hour.

"It's late," he said. "Aren't you expected back?"

The boy jumped to his feet. "Oh, yes! I must be back by nightfall, or they will worry. They do not like my coming here," he confessed.

"Well, let's go," Max said, and at the startled look on Ishtarn's face he added, "I'm coming with you. I've got the urge to see people again. Or—" he looked more closely at Ishtarn "—do you think your people would care to meet a stranger?"

"Oh, yes, sir; they will ask you to the fire and demand your stories," Ishtarn said, an impish grin on his face. "They will not believe you, but they will be delighted. We see few new faces except at marrying time."

The three of them made a tight fit in the small boat, but with Max paddling they crossed the lazy river easily. They beached the boat high on the bank of the opposite shore and followed a well-marked path along the bank and down into a meadow, then across a hill and into a clump of trees. "I have come more often than they know," Ishtarn confided.

Then they were coming down a gentle slope, and before them in the gathering dusk was a herd of goat-like animals which reached out far across the meadow, and nearby was a cluster of tents and cooking fires. Max could see many brightly clad people moving purposefully about in the encampment. Their movements were unguarded; it was a peaceful scene.

Then the wolf's nose rose, and he growled softly. And below them a sudden chorus of barking began.

A man detached himself from among the tents and started up the slope toward them, a long crooked staff in his hand, flowing robes of bright colors swirling about him. Behind him three small, yapping dogs followed closely.

As they grew nearer to each other, Max could make out details of the man's appearance. He was tall, and straight and thin as a rail. But it was not a fragile thinness; Max sensed a wiry strength to the man well before they met. It was in the way he held himself, the way he moved.

The man's hair was white, as were his moustaches and long, flowing beard, and it was impossible to tell whether the color was from the sun or the man's age. His skin was fair like the boy's, but while Ishtarn's was smooth and unmarked, the man's was weathered and lined, the skin of a man long accustomed to the outdoors.

The dogs, short-haired terrierlike animals, hung back now, not wanting to greet the wolf too precipitously. They were silent now, too, while the wolf held only a faint growl in the back of his throat.

The man's eyes darted from Ishtarn to Max, and back again. He seemed pleased to see the boy safe at hand; puzzled by Max's appearance.

Then they met, and Ishtarn, his voice dancing, said, "Maxquest, this is my father, Ishmight!"

Chapter 11

They surrounded him, they stared at him, they whispered about him—several times he heard a dialect he could not completely follow—they touched him and admired him, and then they led him to a fire before the tallest tent, sat him, and fed him. He was Ishmight's guest.

These were a simple folk, nomads who lived in the lowland plains between the rivers, pasturing their flocks and pitching their tents. The winters were mild here—there was rarely snow, they told him; they held an almost superstitious awe of the lands where there was always snow—and they lived a pleasant, uncomplicated life, the monotony punctuated now and then by the elements and the raiders.

But they were shrewd and not unintelligent. In Ishmight Max recognized a keen intellect and a born leader. The man had taken him to his fire and board as guest, but his generosity would not be without some purpose. Max wondered what that might be.

The food was rich and good. The main course was a stew, thick with gravy and goat meat, with various other vegetables and roots added and such herbs and spices as grew wild in the vicinity. The aroma was tantalizing long before he received his portion; the stew bubbled gently in an ancient black pot suspended over the fire from a blackened tripod.

"You come from beyond the mountains, my son tells me," Ismight said, probing gently.

"Yes," Max answered. "From the desert beyond."

There was a chorus of drawn breaths from around the circle, but Ishmight was regarding him keenly, and Max remembered the boy's words: *"They will not believe you, but they will be delighted."*

He pointed at the crude pack beside him. Ishmight had politely and pointedly refrained from asking about it. It held no meat now; only scraps of skin from the toad's belly, the long bones from the leg, gnawed clean by the wolf, and the knives. "That hide came from a beast I killed in the desert," he said, flatly. Let them disbelieve that.

Ishmight reached forward and touched, then fingered, the hide. "Strange leather, this. I have never seen it before."

Max told him of the toad. Ismight nodded wisely. He had heard tales of such creatures.

"The wolf," he asked, "where did you get him?"

Max looked fondly at the wolf, now curled by his feet, gnawing a soup bone tossed him by Ishtarn. "In the desert; I found him in a wild pack. I broke his leg, then set it. He is well trained; he was once another's."

"A trained wolf..." Ishmight mused. "I have never heard of such a thing as that. And yet, he is there for us to see, and we see that it is so." He looked up again, eyes sharp. "And here, too, are you. You are an unusual man, Maxquest. You look like no one in this land; you are dressed like a beast. You carry little, and travel with a wolf by your side. And you come from the desert. Who are you?"

Max considered the question. It would be easy to palm off any answer upon this man, or none at all. He owed no explanation for himself beyond that which appearance made for him. Yet there was something about this man which made him want to trust him, made him feel a need for him to understand.

"I come from another world," Max said at last. "I have come to seek a woman."

The other sat quietly and pondered the statement. "You came to the desert," he said, in a question which was not spoken as a question, but as confirmation.

"I could not choose my destination," Max said.

"And you walked out of the desert."

Max nodded.

"I know of no one who has ever done that before, and only stories of those who have ventured beyond the mountains. Their curiosity was the end of them...." He let his voice trail off in reflection. Then: "And you seek a woman. Any woman?" The eyes were very sharp now.

Max felt the brush of fear. He might have said too much; he had no way of knowing what superstitions these people held. In his admission that he was not of this world, would they think him a demon, come to seize a bride from among them? He sensed a withdrawal from around the circle, and other bright eyes upon him.

"No," he said. "My woman—a woman of my world. My enemies cast her here, to force me to follow, so that they might be rid of me."

"Are you then an important man in your world?"

"I...never thought of myself that way, but to my enemies...." Max paused to let his mind grasp the idea more fully. "I suppose I was."

"And your woman—have you found sign of her?"

"None—yet."

"The desert?"

"I don't know." Max passed a weary hand over his temples. "I can only hope. You've heard nothing, then, of a strange woman, perhaps coming out of the mountains?"

"None."

And Max knew that he had reached as far as this trail would take him. He had expected nothing; he knew no one had preceded him over the mountain road, and that was the most direct path into these people's land.

"But they may know in the north," Ishmight said.

"*The raiders...*" It was a whisper which passed around the circle like wind through the grass.

Max waited.

"Yes," said the other, slowly. "You might find her among the raiders."

"Who are they?"

"Rassanala and his men. They have built a fortress, near where the East River forks. They are a callous lot. They steal goats, and sometimes slaves, from among the plains people. They ride great animals, and are very swift."

"Have they caused any real damage?" Max asked. His curiosity was balanced between politeness and real interest; he was not at all certain of the likelihood that a gang of ruffians and raiders would have Fran. And yet, if someone strange, an attractive young woman, appeared in this land—would this draw them?

"They have taken only scattered flocks and their shepherds," Ishmight said, "from among us, at any rate. Others have not always fared as well. The tribe of Jermiad was trapped and taken whole. But they did not have our weapons...a crossbow fares quite well against a sword, if one takes advantage of its range...." A smile curved his lips bleakly. Then, as if sensing Max's thoughts, "You could not go to them openly. They welcome no strangers, recognize no traders. What they wish, they take, and travelers become slaves."

They fed Max, and then they bedded him. They gave him skins, a place in Ishmight's tent, and a companion. She was a young girl—Max wondered if she could be over fifteen—already swelling with womanhood. She was short, slender, and long blonde hair fell to her waist when she released it from its braids.

Max was embarrassed. His long and silent sojourn in the desert had pitted him against elemental nature, demanding of him all his strength and thought. When he thought of sex, he did so as he remembered Fran: part of another, far less savage world.

The girl's name was Bajra, and he did not want her. It was not, he told himself, that he was simply being faithful to the memory of Fran—a vague distrust nagged in his occluded memories of the dreams the cactus had brought him: a feeling of obscure guilt and shame—nor that she was too young, either. But somehow it was both of these and something else. The thought slipped through his mind that he was a knight on a quest, and he dismissed it as an adolescent fantasy, but there was something to that, as well.

"Forgive me," Max said to Ishmight. "I am a stranger here, and your guest. But I'd rather—" He gestured to the open tent flap, and Ishmight understood.

"You've slept too often under the stars," he said, and Max nodded. The girl, Bajra, stood silently, combing her fair hair.

Max took the proffered skins and robes out onto the open grass. The air had cooled with the coming of night, and the grass was wet with dew. He drew a strong breath. Ishmight had been right, too. The confines of the tent, with its strong scents of oiled and perfumed bodies and still hanging cooking odors, had led to his discomfiture as well. And there had been the lack of privacy. For himself he did not mind, but he did not fancy lying close to another man's marriage bed. It was all in one's culture, he guessed. Ishtarn had seemed unperturbed.

He'd settled himself among the furs and was sleepily luxuriating in a comfort he'd grown unused to, when there was a rustle of sound close by, he felt a tug on the robes over him, and then a soft body curled against his own.

"It will be much warmer," a voice said close to his ear. "It grows cooler before dawn." An arm encircled his chest, and he felt her face burrow into his neck and shoulders, her long hair pleasantly tickling against his skin. He fell into an easy sleep.

In the morning she was still there, and Max stared down at

her small and innocent face. The first rays of dawn lit the camp. No one yet stirred. Had he taken too much for granted? She was so young...perhaps here people slept together for comfort. He remembered something Ishmight had said the night before—that one did not marry within one's own tribe. When one reached the proper age, tribes met and exchanged partners in marriage. It was a gala occasion, celebrated with much feasting and dancing.

It was a eugenic law, Max realized. The tribes were too small, and showed remarkable inbreeding as it was. They would not wish to encourage more. So if unmarried boys and girls slept together, it would not necessarily be for sex; indeed, that might be prohibited. He wondered if normally Bajra slept with Ishtarn. The thought piqued a point of jealousy he'd not known he had, and he angrily suppressed it. That, surely, was no business of his. He stared at the open innocence on the sleeping girl's face.

And yet...if inbreeding was a problem, new stock would be welcomed with open arms. In which case...Had Ishmight sent the girl out here to him? What did they expect of him, anyway?

His feelings toward these people were friendly. They had taken him in and given him hospitality. They were good-hearted people, and he found himself liking them easily. Ismight was a shrewd man. And if he wanted to introduce a strain of thick-bodied, tall, dark men into his tribe, could Max blame him? He chuckled to himself. It was no such terrible thing they might be asking of him....And yet—

Her eyes opened. She looked up at him questioningly.

"Bajra." Max asked in a whisper, close to her ear, "what do you expect of me?"

Her answer was simple and to the point. "To be a man to me," she said softly.

"You know I seek another?"

"I do not ask that you marry me." She looked deep into his eyes. "I know you will not stay here long."

"You want to have a child by me?"

"There is that, yes," she said. But her look told him that a child was not the only reason.

He smiled. "Can you be sure you would?"

Her answer was sober. "Yes; that is why I was selected."

"And did this please you?"

"I did not know you then," she said, and raised her face, lips ready, eyes closing.

That morning Max went out into the fields with Ishtarn. Their ostensible task was to act as a roving guard against a possible surprise raid. But much of the day was spent while Ishtarn taught Max the use of the crossbow he had been given.

It was an easy instrument to master; Max practiced at successively greater distances from a marked tree trunk, the tree growing considerably more marked as the day wore on.

The crossbow did not vary greatly from those he had seen in the Museum back home, except that it was made wholly of wood. The bow was thick and heavy; made, Ishtarn told him, of fire-hardened wood from a tree which grew only to the north. It had required several dangerous missions to procure enough of the right wood.

The bow was fitted in a stock which was notched to hold it. A pegged lever lay along the length of the stock, and when raised and pulled back served to draw the bowstring back and cock it. The stock was grooved and bored, beyond the bow, for the shaft. The bow was set below the level of the shaft in the stock, since they had not wanted to weaken it by notching or grooving it, and this meant that the bowstring had to ride above its natural plane. The stock between the bow and the cocking trigger was kept to a high polish by the rubbing of the string, and Ishtarn said the strings wore out frequently.

It was a powerful weapon, more powerful than the smaller one he'd taken away from the boy the day before. It was difficult even for a man of Max's strength to cock. But it would sink a shaft through a man at 500 yards, Ishtarn told him proudly.

The day went easily enough. Max found the boy eager to tell him of his people and their customs, and even more eager to hear more tales of the desert, and, as he put it, "the world beyond." Max told him little of his home world, sensing that it would sound too much like the fantasies of the cactus to the boy.

The wolf stayed near them, and Max found himself regarding the beast affectionately. He was a valued partner far more than a pet, and had grown to become something of a fixture in his life, Max realized.

The wolf provided the one incident of the afternoon, when he disappeared into a nearby copse of trees in a dip of land and reappeared soon after with a small, squirrel-like animal. He dropped it at Max's feet and went bounding away again.

"What is that?" asked Ishtarn in surprise. "He has brought you a dead muney."

Max laughed. "He has brought me my lunch. He often hunted for me when we were coming down off the mountains." And, he remembered, earlier he had found grubs for the wolf. It had been a reciprocal arrangement.

"Did you eat such animals?" asked the boy, his eyes wide.

"Little else," Max replied, picking up the dead creature. He found his saliva running. He was hungry, and the fresh blood smelled good. He fished out his knife and began skinning it.

"You have no fire," the boy said.

Max looked up, startled. "You know, I'd forgotten that—I've got a thing now that I can make fires with. Found it in that house, just before you showed up."

"But what did you do before you found it?" Ishtarn asked.

Max finished skinning the muney and eyed it cheerfully. "Why," he said, "I ate them raw." He sank his teeth into the warm and tender flesh of the small animal.

He wiped the blood from his mouth with the back of his hand. "It's quite good. Want some?"

Ishtarn stepped back, his face showing his surprise and disgust. "No, please."

Max regarded the boy thoughtfully for a moment, still chewing. He swallowed. "You know," he said, "living in the desert is not a story-teller's adventure."

Understanding came into Ishtarn's eyes then.

The raiders hit them in the dark of night.

Max had been asleep, nestled in his furs with Bajra, their nude bodies intertwined in easy intimacy.

When she had come to his bed again that night, he had found himself anticipating it, his thoughts turning unbidden to the moments with her that early morning. He had known then that she had been a virgin, and he had felt clumsy and inadequate, her virginity somehow transforming the act into one in which he found himself inexperienced, and she had taken the upper hand, leading, guiding him. It had surprised him. He had thought about it later, while busying himself with the crossbow and targets, Ishtarn's chatter passing over his thoughts without disturbing them. This was a different culture, he reminded himself. People thought differently here. It was not so much in their obvious actions as in their more subtle customs and mores—in their attitudes toward sex, marriage, and procreation. In a way, he envied them. Bajra would make one of them a fine wife some day And her husband would be proud of his adopted child, the one with black hair and broad shoulders. They would speak of the man who'd come from the desert—a god perhaps? Did these people have gods?—and left his seed with them to help them grow stronger.

Or was he allowing his ego a too-free rein?

But when he had returned to the camp that evening, he had

looked for her, and when he saw her their glances crossed, their eyes held one another. And he waited, in anticipation, for the night.

It had been very different that night with them; less exploratory and instead a willing, eager partnership. This slender girl had waited for him, he realized, to bring out in her this moving, exulting sensuality, to awaken her instincts. Max felt troubled when it was over, and she lay already asleep in his arms. He felt the subtle stirrings of emotions, reaching out to her, establishing a bond with her. Her slight but soft body nestled against him, and he told himself: this is a real person. She has feelings, emotions. She is young, and you have awakened her deepest feelings, Max. Can you stride off across the plains and leave her?

What was your bond to Fran? That you'd slept with her? That emotional ties had formed between you two—and you found yourself caught in that which you called love, not knowing a better word for it, or a better meaning for the word?

Can you love two women, Max? Can your love for Fran still be real while you lie here with Bajra? To whom do you owe your loyalties?

He slipped into an uneasy sleep filled with disturbing dreams. Once his arms tightened convulsively around Bajra, and she turned in her sleep and kissed him, and the tenseness left him again.

It was after midnight; the larger moon had set behind the mountains hours earlier, and the small one, full now and its tiny disk almost more like a star, was high in the sky. The stars wove a jeweled tapestry.

The fires had been banked and now burned low. The camp was asleep.

Then, suddenly, all was chaos.

Max could not remember where he was at first. A soft, feminine body was curled against his, and he thought for a moment it was Fran. But he was surrounded by alien sounds— sounds they'd never known in far away New York. Heavy hooves beat the ground around them, and his ears were filled with triumphant shouts and startled cries.

A rider on a great beast pounded past Ishmight's tent, and the beast kicked up the fire, scattering burning embers onto and into the tent. The fabric of the tent caught fire immediately, and bright flames leapt up to illumine the scene.

Bajra was clinging to his arm, her face distended with shock and fear. Her mouth was open, but if she was screaming he could not hear it. Breaking loose from her, he rolled over and grabbed for the crossbow and shafts.

He climbed to his knees, his tanned bare body still too close to the ground to be noticed by the raiders. He stopped and struggled the crossbow taut, and then slipped in a shaft. Cocked and loaded, he waited for a clear target.

"*Max!*" Bajra screamed.

Without taking his eyes from the scene before him, Max pushed the girl back, motioned to her to lie under the covers. Perhaps she would escape notice.

Then another rider swept toward them on the back of a shadowy steed. The man was leaning low iin his saddle, swinging a sword back and forth, ripping tents and collapsing them.

The sounds beat against them, an unholy din that at once both crept up his legs from the ground and pierced his ears, but Max held steady, and aimed carefully. He pulled the trigger.

Chapter 12

The shaft passed through the beast's neck and into its rider's chest. Man and animal gave a horrible cry together. But Max was not aware of them.

Without waiting to see the results of his shot, he fumbled again with the bow, cursing its cumbersomeness. If it had been lighter he might not have its long-range striking power, but what did that matter now? He needed greater speed.

Many tents were burning now, their glow lighting the camp, sparks flying in the night wind. Max slapped at one which lit upon his back. He shot another raider from his saddle. The shaft passed clean through the man.

Max was on his feet now, loading and refiring with machine-like regularity. He paid no attention to the others in the camp; he was only dimly aware of the struggling women loading and passing crossbows to their men, of children stamping at the burning tents, and of others struggling to free themselves of the collapsed folds of brightly colored coth—some of it now burning a bright funeral pyre around them. His attention was focused solely upon the night raiders, the shadowy figures who rode back and forth through the camp, swinging swords and thrusting firebrands at yet unburning tents. There was no dearth of targets.

There was a growl that somehow pierced the wall of sound and then a snarl from behind him. He half turned to see the wolf attacking a man on foot. The man was dressed in leather—one of the raiders. He turned his back on them and went on with his loading and shooting. The wolf had had the man by the neck; he would need no assistance there.

The flames leapt high about the camp, now, and Max had no

difficulty in picking out the swirl of riding raiders from the half-dressed and bedraggled defenders. The invaders had swords, the tribesmen crossbows.

On an open battlefield it might have been a very different story, for there the nomads would have had the benefit of range. But their crossbows were hunting weapons; the raiders' swords were battle weapons. And although the raiders were outnumbered, they held the upper hand. Max could read quite clearly the way this night's battle would go.

His shafts were exhausted, and almost gratefully he threw the bow down, grabbing the sword of the man his wolf had killed.

It was a crude and primitive sword. It had a blunt point, and although both edges had once been cutting edges, they were now nicked and turned. From the heft of it, the sword was beaten iron.

The raiders were dismounting now, and were dragging struggling women and girls from their tents and tossing them over their steeds. With the wolf at his back, Max leapt forward, swinging his sword in a great arc at the nearest raider.

The sword chopped into the man's shoulder with a jolt that ran up Max's arm. The raider's arm fell cleanly away, its hand still spasmically clutching a young girl. The girl's mouth was wide, and she held an endless scream. She did not seem to know what was happening to her.

The taste of blood ran deep in him now. Max felt the bite of the sword as he swung it again and again, wading deeper into the throng of raiders. Shooting a crossbow was like sitting, detached, before a target gallery. He had been plunking at moving targets then; now he was among them. He laughed wildly as he swung and slashed.

Later he wondered at himself, at the primitive emotions he had uncovered in himself in this world. But he did not question then the pleasure it gave him to strike out physically at his attackers. It was a release he'd long awaited, ever since his growing frustration with the slippery Others. Now he was like a madman, slashing and cutting, laughing and screaming, blood and sweat gleaming on his naked body, fighting as they must never have seen a plainsman fight.

Then, suddenly, the riders were in the midst of the fray again, their huge steeds trampling tribesman and raider alike among those on foot. One of the raiders came up on Max from behind, and he felt the thud of the animal's hooves on the turf, but had no chance to turn. The rider swung his sword, and it struck Max's head.

Only the wolf saved him then. The wolf had been at his back, protecting him, and when the rider brought his sword down, the fierce animal leapt for the man's arm. It was not enough to stop the blow, but the wolf's grip on the man's arm turned it, and his sword struck Max with its flat instead of its edge.

It was a stunning blow, and Max fell into a great reaching well of blackness.

As he fell, another rider leaned low in his saddle and swept up the stumbling figure, dragging him by the hair and one arm, up and across the steed's pommel.

The pain in his scalp sent bright flashes to the back of his eyes, and Max became conscious again long enough to see his wolf leap at his abductor—and to see the proud beast slashed and beheaded by the man's sword. Then he fell back into a long unconsciousness.

He felt seasick. When he awoke he found himself lying, face down, over a great leathery, heaving thing. The night was still dark; he could see little, but he knew he was moving. He was trussed and draped over a foul-smelling animal, and every jolt of its steps hit him in the stomach. He was sick. He vomited.

Overhead he heard a voice utter a sudden curse, and then he knew that the shadowy object to his right, now dripping with the remains of his last meal, was a man's leg and foot in a stirrup.

The animal jogged with a rolling gait. Max felt himself about to be sick again, and a dry spasm passed over him, ending in a retching noise that was loud in his own ears. Then he saw the foot rise out of the stirrup and deliver a ringing kick to his head.

It was a grueling ordeal. Several times he regained consciousness and lost it again. He had no idea of the passage of time; only that at some point the endless nightmare became one with the inferno of day, the sun carving cruelly into his back.

His arms were lashed behind his back and his feet tied together. He was naked. He might as well have been a sack of grain. There was a total indignity to his position, and it was sometimes accented when he felt the touch of curiously gentle hands, probing.

As the heat built with the day, he found himself sweating freely, the sweat rolling down his back, around his neck, and across his face. It trickled into his mouth, his nose, his eyes. It tasted salty, it tickled maddeningly, it stung.

He could see little but the side of the beast he was on, his captor's leg and foot, and the ground passing below. The beast's hide was a leathery yellow and streaked with dust, sweat, blood,

Then suddenly the riders were in the midst of the fray.

and vomit. Its odor was decidely unpleasant.

Black spots swam before his eyes and occasionally occluded his vision. He had no way of knowing how long these periods of semi-consciousness were, nor did he care. He wished only for an end to this hell.

Yet, when that end came, he was unconscious again, and his first awareness of change was when he found himself lying upon hard ground, water drenching him.

His hands and feet were free, he discovered, but he could hardly move his limbs. They felt heavy and distant from him. Water splashed over him again, and he opened his eyes.

He was in an open stockade. High on the walls above guards patrolled ceaselessly. Here on the open ground below were the prisoners. They were all tribesmen; many he recognized. A girl was standing over him with a wooden bucket. Bajra.

"You are awake?" she asked. "You are all right?"

He lifted a numb hand and rubbed his face with it, groggily. His hand felt bloated and unreal, not his own.

"I found you and untied you," she said, and there was strength and pride in her eyes. He looked around again, taking in the ragged, tattered lot of the prisoners, and then returning his eyes to the girl.

She was half naked; she had fastened a ragged piece of cloth around her waist. It was the first time he had actually looked upon her body; before they had been under covers or in the dark. She stood small but straight, and without shame. As he had known it was, her figure was slight, slender. She was still a girl, and had not yet completed her growth. Her breasts were small and high on her chest; their tips had the suggestion of an upward tilt. They were too small to have any sag. Her torso curved down over a muscled stomach and in for an impossibly tiny waist. The swell of her hips was yet tentative, still somewhat boyish. Her hair was a tumble and uncombed. It fell in a golden mat down her back and over one shoulder. There were smudges of dried blood and perhaps soot on her face and arms, although it was obvious that she had tried to wash them off.

She held her head up, but her small lips trembled, and he knew the effort she was making to be brave, to be the adult she wished to be thought.

She had tied a similar rag around his own waist, he discovered, and she had done her best to wash and clean him. He still felt the stickiness of sweat, but he was lying in the sun, and that could not be helped.

"I saw them seize you," she was saying, "You fought

magnificiently."

"Ishmight? Ishtarn?" Max asked.

"Dead," she said soberly. A thin tear moved slowly down one cheek. "They killed him, because he had resisted them—to teach him, us, a lesson. The plains people must learn to pay tribute—they say."

Max felt himself moved. Ishtarn, Ishmight—son and father—he had not known them long, but he found himself missing them strongly. And now—what would become of their people, of their plans, of Bajra?

"This is the prisoners' pen," she explained. "We will be sorted out, some of the women for Rassanala's harem, some of us to be servants in the city, and the men to become servants, slaves, and...other things. You, I do not know.... They fear you as a fighter, and would have killed you, but one of the men—Rassanala's son, some say—wanted you and took you. Now, I do not know. A slave, perhaps, and hard labor. Or...I do not know."

"But you, Bajra?"

She shrugged. "The harem, if I am lucky. A scullery, if I am not. Women they need. It is the men they fear and distrust, and...use."

"What do you mean?"

"These people, they—I do not know how to say it. They are unnatural. They do not think as we do. They...they breed with their women, but they get no pleasure from them."

He remembered the hands questing his body, and understood.

They were in Rassanala's fortress. The people who lived here called it City Rassanala, after their leader; and, from Bajra's description of it, Max was reminded of the European feudal village of the middle ages. There was a great outer wall, which served as the city's outer defense ring, and within that wall a fantastic conglomeration of two- to four-story buildings distributed almost entirely without plan, twisting narrow streets and alleys, only the few broadest paved with stone, winding among them. Rassanala's own dwelling was not quite a castle, but constituted an inner line of defense. Max wondered if it might not serve as protection against the people of the city, as well as those without.

They were fed slop in troughs, like animals, and Max was glad for even that; his stomach had taken a cruel beating and the simple gruel was easily digestible. In the back of his mind was the memory of fresh blood, however...and in his present frame of mind, he would not object to the raider's blood.

What was happening to him? He had felt it among the nomads; his uneasiness in clothing, his claustrophobia in the tent. And, much as he had enjoyed their cooked food, he had still eaten the fresh-killed muney his wolf had brought him, and with great relish. Even among the tribesmen, he was a savage.

Here, now, he was even more so. The fighting had brought it out in him—his blood lust, his anger and passion. He remembered the sight of the faithful wolf, defending him to the end, its head with still snapping jaws cloven free by the sweep of a sword. These raiders—decadent, vultures preying upon honest men— the thought of them brought a black rage upon him, where it smouldered and built from within. He no longer talked with Bajra, and the girl ceased her chattering and sat close by him with downcast eyes.

Late in the afternoon, overseers with great bullwhips came into the stockade. They cracked their whips over the conquered, bringing them down upon those they felt might still offer resistance. One lash laid Max flat on the ground, stunned, but still conscious.

His inner rage reached a white heat. He had passed beyond the moment of black passion into the fine temper of cold and inhuman deliberation. Without rising from his prone position, he watched....

The people were cowed now. They had seen friends, relatives, members of their own family wounded or killed; they had been taken captive and treated with less kindness than they'd have treated their own goats. They were tired, physically and emotionally exhausted. They were cowed.

The overseers passed among them, contemptuous, and drew forth the women, separating them from their men and driving each group with many cracks of the whips, to opposite walls of the stockade. Max was grasped by the hair and yanked to his feet, to stumble quietly among the other men. But a hooded look in his eyes caused even his fellow prisoners to draw back a little from him. There was a look about him of one who is not quite sane.

Then, with the callousness of men inspecting prize cattle, the overseers stripped the women and began ranking them by their physical beauty. The women held their heads high, their expressions proud and distant, as they were subjected to indifferent indignities. Among the men around him Max heard, like the distant murmur of waves upon the seashore, the growing mutters of rage. These men were watching their wives, sisters, daughters.

The overseers were sorting the women into two groups, the

younger, prettier ones for the harem, the others for menial servant tasks. There were only a few overseers standing in the middle of the courtyard between them and the muttering men, but these guards held great woven bullwhips, some as much as ten feet long. Their snap was as sharp as a pistol shot, and their whiplash could mark a man for life—if it did not kill him first.

Beyond the groups of women and the overseers stood the gate of the stockade. It had been opened when they'd entered, and remained not quite shut. Such carelessness would cost them dearly, Max decided.

The routine was nearing completion. It was obviously old hat to the guards, and they were bored. Once in a while one would toy with his whip, snapping it in the air as if to re-demonstrate his virility, but they were less watchful now, preferring to spend their gazes upon the group of women being lined up for the harem. Jokes and obscene jests passed among them.

The sun cut sharply over the stockade wall from the west. No breeze stirred. Dust hung heavy in the air, individual motes caught, impaled, by the beams of sunlight. Rassanala's men worked with the bored ease of long accomplishment. The smell of human waste and sweat permeated the stockade. One of the guards held his hand to his nose and grinned at another. Max heard a phrase which sounded like, " . . . those cattle . . ."

He dropped suddenly to his knees and then, still crouched over, darted out into the open.

With desert-hardened sinews, he thrust his hand, fingers outstretched tight and stiff, up into the guard's solar plexus. He could feel the muscles under the guard's still unbroken skin tearing loose from his ribcage as he angled up under the man's left ribs.

It was fast—too quickly done for Max even to catch the man's startled expression as his face turned a sudden deep red, his tongue bulged from his mouth, and he dropped, dead of a ruptured heart, to the ground.

In that long but fleeting moment of attack, Max heard no sound, felt no passage of time. The universe had narrowed down to a sunlit spot some five feet square, in which had stood only he and the guard. Now, as he snatched for the guard's whip, the sounds suddenly reached him again, and as he looked up he saw the stockade yard boiling with shouts and confusion.

His attack upon the guard had galvanized the others. They had needed only his example to set them off. They outnumbered the guards and overseers and now they swarmed over them, their own frustrated anger driving them into the guards to strike and claw and choke and kill with bare hands and fists. Shouts of alarm went up from the guards, but were quickly choked off by the grimly determined plainsmen. And as each guard fell, his whip was snatched up by one of the prisoners.

Snapping his own whip angrily, Max aimed for the overseers. The women had drawn back from them, leaving them an exposed group. There were six of the men, each dressed in rich—and probably stolen—fabrics, some of which Max was sure he'd seen before in Ishmight's camp.

A bloodthirsty scream split the air, but Max was not aware that it was his own as he cracked his whip into the massed overseers.

His first snap of the whip cut down their leader, blood running freely from a gash torn in his throat. Then Max was cutting and lashing the others, and they were splitting, running, heading for the open gate.

Max moved to cut them off. If they reached the gate, if they got through it and got it closed again—!

One of them still had a whip. It was shorter, but Max sensed his strategy. He would attempt to tangle it with Max's and wrest the whip from him. Max grinned. That sword could cut both ways.

The other swung his whip back and started to whip it forward, when one of the girls from the harem group darted forward, arms outthrust.

It was Bajra, Max saw, and the whip wrapped itself around her arms, cracking nastily. But she caught at it and yanked. The overseer was thrown off balance. Max cut him down.

The other prisoners were swarming forward now, and Max found himself and Bajra in an eddy around which the others swirled in their push for the gate.

From the corner of his eyes, he saw them gain the gate and mass their way through it, but his attention was on the girl. The whip had dropped from her arms, and where it had been there were now fiery welts, tiny droplets of blood rising from them in spots. The young girl was nude, but Max was not aware of that as he pulled her toward him and held her and kissed her. Then, roughly, he pushed her from him, turned her, and started her for the gate. "Hurry," he told her, "this is our chance."

He stooped to pick up the whip he'd dropped, and then the universe descended upon his skull, and he knew no more.

Chapter 13

Max awoke to find himself lying on a great bed. He was lying between silken covers, and he found himself staring at a canopy of orange overhead.

He had a splitting headache, and when he attempted to sit up a great throbbing hit him at his temples, each throb a hammer-blow against his aching brain. He let himself back down again, very carefully, and waited for his heart to slow again.

He had seen something of the room he was in, though, and it surprised him.

He had been struck down in the dust of the stockade; now he was in an opulently furnished apartment. The walls were of wood paneling, with drapes and tapestries hanging here and there. The bed was huge, large enough to accommodate several Maxes. Nearby was a small table. On it were a cut crystal pitcher and a heavy matching glass. The pitcher held a darkish fluid. Max struggled to his elbows again, this time less abruptly. With shaking hands, he poured less than half a glass. Then, propping himself up against the pillows, he took a sip.

It was a wine of some sort, and from its aftertaste he suspected it was made from honey. It was spiced, and the cool fragrances seemed to clear his head somewhat. He began to take a more detailed interest in his surroundings.

The room was well-furnished, but there was little that could be moved or used as a weapon. Cupboards and cabinets were a part of the paneled walls.

As he shifted about, he discovered that he was again without clothes, but also that he had been bathed and rubbed down with perfumed oils. He held one forearm to his nose and sniffed. It had a peppery fragrance.

Despite the bed and the care that had been spent upon him, he ached. He ached all over. His muscles felt strained and exhausted. When he'd lifted the pitcher of wine, it had taken a great effort not to spill it; he'd felt as weak as a baby.

Still, it would not do to remain too long abed. Carefully, mindful of the throbbing still at his temples, he swung his feet to the carpeted floor and eased himself erect.

First he checked the door. As he'd expected, it was locked. Then he began prowling the rest of the room. He poked behind each hanging drape or tapestry, finding only bare solid wall. In the end he found himself before the window.

It was a large window, and beyond it he could see a balcony that ran along the side of the wall and beyond, to his left. But the window was heavily barred, with wrought iron that looked vaguely ornamental but was no less functional.

Dusk had fallen upon the city beyond, and he could make out only rooftops and silhouettes. His window faced west, and in the distance he could see the yellow glow of the sun which had itself dropped behind the distant mountains.

For a few long moments he thought, then, of the desert where the sun would still be shining now and where—if he were still there—he would now be in the midst of his afternoon chores and beginning preparations for the nightly hunt. He felt a momentary pang of nostalgia. Then he recalled his purpose in being here—in being on this very world.

Fran. Did she indeed exist here? What a cruel jest it would be if the Others had sent him to a different world—one which had never known her.

Fran. Why was he hunting her? He had lost his powers; there could be no return. Her image was faded in his mind now, the memory of the elfin Bajra far stronger. But yet....

Fran would be an alien here, like himself—if indeed she was here at all. Bajra—had she and her people escaped?—knew an ordered life here, and this was her world. She had little curiosity about it.

But the memory of Bajra occluded that of Fran.

There was a click from the door, and then it opened.

Max turned and stared through the increasing gloom of the room.

A man had entered, and now he relocked the door, straightening quickly to face Max and drop a key into a pocket of his robes.

Max had no memory of seeing the man before, but he

108

recognized his type. The man was tall and thin, blond like all the people who lived on this plain, but with a deeply tanned skin and, Max was later to note, black eyes. His hair, which fell to his shoulders, was not the white-blond of Ishmight or his people, either, but rather a darker color bleached by the sun in streaks. The man also wore a neatly trimmed goatee, but it did not strengthen his face. His cheeks were faintly hollowed, but any ascetic look which that might have produced was offset by the loose fullness of his lips. He had the weak look of the pampered; his mouth seemed to fall naturally into a pout.

But he was a big man, a tall man whose thinness did not fully conceal a wiry strength.

"You are awake, I see. Recovered?"

Max remained silent and regarded the man.

The other laughed, exposing decayed teeth. "You needn't fear me, fellow. I am the reason you are still alive." He moved forward and reached out, his hand brushing Max's arm lightly. "I liked the looks of you. Very dark, very handsome."

Max still said nothing.

"I saved your life!" the man said with sudden emphasis. "You are mine." He licked his lips in an unconcious gesture. "You will serve me in all the ways that I command, Dark One. I control your life."

"And just what is it that you want of me?" Max asked, breaking his silence at last. But he knew.

The answer was shockingly direct. The man reached out and caressed him intimately. "Pleasure," the man said.

Max found himself shaking almost uncontrollably as he suddenly turned away from the man. "What makes you think I would cooperate with you?" he asked.

He felt the other move up closely behind him, one hand patting his buttocks, the other curving around his waist. "Pleasure," the man repeated.

Suddenly Max reached for the arm that was encircling him, grabbed it with both hands, lifted it over his shoulder, and then snapped his body down and forward.

With a startled scream, the other flipped over his shoulders and slammed onto the floor on his back.

The man was stunned, breathless, but not out. Max picked up the wine pitcher and brought it down on the man's head. Wine sloshed over his face and mixed with the welling blood. But his eyes did not close. They stared up, sightlessly, gaze fixed upon eternity.

Max stared down at him. But somehow his death was only

an abstraction. Max could not equate this limp figure with a human being. Then he began stripping the dead man of his clothes and donning them on his own huskier frame.

In one pocket he found the key, a large, crude, and clumsily ornate thing of beaten iron. He unlocked the door and eased it open.

The hallway was lit by candles spaced at intervals on the walls. There was no one in sight. He pulled the door shut and locked it, and then began picking his way stealthily down the hall.

He was in Rassanala's castle, that was obvious. No other building in this ragtag city would be or could be this richly appointed.

He stopped an old man on the steps. The man bore a tray with the remains of a meal upon it. Max helped himself to an apple-like fruit. The old man he seized by his beard.

"Where is the harem, old man?" he asked roughly.

"Why, why," the man quavered, "that is a place forbidden to all but the Duke Rassanala and his officers."

"I am growing deaf," Max said. "Tell me again: where is the harem?"

The look in his eyes warned the old man. He told him. Max left the man in an alcove behind a drape, trussed up and gagged with his own clothes.

The harem was not hard to find. There were few people about in the castle, and most of them servants. Max was well dressed, and in the gloom of the flickering candles, he could pass easily for one who belonged. It was important to walk proudly, without stealth, to act as though one belong where one was. The servants would not question him.

The harem was a separate set of chambers, sealed off from the main part of the castle by an anteroom locked at both ends. Max found that his key worked quite satisfactorily on both doors—either the locks were quite crude here, or perhaps only important people were allowed keys which would unlock all doors; it didn't matter—and the guard who sat in the anteroom was fat and old and required only a moment to deal with.

On the other side of the door Max found simply a continuation of the corridor. Visions of eastern harems as they'd been pictured by a multitude of cartoonists had been running through his mind, but there was nothing to suggest anything like that here.

Uncertainly, he made his way down the hall, past a series of

110

closed doors on either side. Once he heard a baby bawling behind one door, and he hesitated. Then he pushed on.

Suddenly a door ahead opened, and a young girl came out. She had been turning away from him, but the sight of him must have caught the corner of her eye, for she whirled and stared at him her eyes flashing angrily.

"You!" she demanded imperiously. "What do you think you're doing here?"

Max smiled. "I was just waiting for you."

"What?" The girl stepped back a step.

"I'd like to talk to you." He gestured at the door she'd just stepped through. "Let's go inside."

The girl backed another step, and Max added, "I'm not here to cause you trouble. I need to know about a girl they might have here."

"Who are you?"

Max turned his back on her and opened the door to her room. Without replying, he walked into the room and sat down on a chair. After a moment's hesitation the girl followed him back into the room and sat down on another chair opposite.

The room was not so luxurious as the one he had awakened in, but it would do, Max decided. It had a more lived-in look, as though the girl had invested it with something of her own personality. There were small trinkets scattered here and there, and pictures, some crudely drawn, upon the walls. The bed had no canopy, but was comfortably large.

The girl herself was tall, five-eight Max estimated, and blonde. Her skin coloring was of the nomads, and Max guessed she'd been captured on an earlier raid. She was attractive, but without the youthful beauty of Bajra. Her face was long and looked drawn.

"I am Max Quest," Max told her. "I come from the desert, beyond the western mountains." A look of startled surprise flooded the girl's eyes for a moment; then she masked them again.

"I come, seeking a woman," Max said. "She would've come from the west, I think. She would be unusual among your people—or here. Like me, she had black hair."

Again there was that flicker of knowledge in the girl's eyes, but she said only, "Why do you seek her? What is she to you?"

"We were to be married, once," Max said. "Then she was kidnapped. I have followed for a long way."

"She is your woman? What is her name?"

Max felt his blood quickening. She *knew!* There was a certain knowledge in him then—this girl knew of Fran!

"Fran," he said. He half rose. "She is here?"

The girl regarded him coolly. Then she nodded. "She is here. They brought her here from the raid on the West River some days ago. She has become Rassanala's favorite. He is fascinated by her." She spoke contemptuously, and Max with a flash of insight realized that she was jealous.

"Where is she now?" Max asked.

"The last I heard, she was with old Kashnath," the girl said. "But I do not keep track of her movements."

Max considered this. Fran was here; his quest was ended. It was suddenly disconcerting. Now that he had found her, what next? Another, deeper thought troubled him. He had changed much since he had first arrived in this world. Had Fran also? And if so—in what way? This harem—how would it have affected her?

"You were captured in a raid too, were you not?" Max asked.

"Yes—long ago. I was only a young girl then."

"You don't miss your people?"

"My people? I don't miss their way of life, if that is what you mean. Look about you—I live here. This is my room, my apartment. It is beautiful, is it not? I live in a favored position; I am a consort to the Duke himself. I eat well, I have fine clothes. How can this be compared with herding smelly goats, living in the dust in tattered tents, wearing worn rags for clothes?"

Max was about to contradict her picture of the nomad life, but he paused. She did not know he did not belong here; there was no point in betraying the fact. And perhaps she had come from a poorer tribe—although he was willing to bet that if it had been, Rassanala was the cause of that.

"This Kashrath—who is he?"

The girl started at him, puzzled for a moment that he should not know this. "You have not met Kashrath? I am surprised. He has a great curiosity about the land from which you come."

"I'm newly arrived," Max said wryly.

"He is the Duke's advisor. He can read the firmaments and forecast the future. He tells the weather and finds omens for the raids."

"I see." An old fraud, posing as the local astrologer, then. "And where can I find him? I think he would like to see me."

Kashrath was an old man, his dark face lined and worn, his eyes watery. He had once been tall, but now his bones fell into a perpetual stoop. He was a garrulous old man as well, and he welcomed Max without questioning his position here in the

Castle Rassanala.

"My, yes," the old man said, "from the desert, you say? How very marvelous. Never knew a man to survive long, the other side of the mountains.

"I've a mind to think on Tanashoth, he who was the Rassanala's father...much as the Duke would rather forget it..." he essayed a dry wheezing chuckle "...but I've a memory that goes back far beyond *his* diaper pins....

"Yes, uhmmm, Tanashoth...led an expedition across the mountains, he did...and for what? Eh?" The old man cocked an eye at the impatient Max.

"Followed the road, he did, for days on end. And when he come back, now, what did he have?" He chuckled. "Nothing. Not a thing. Come out of the desert, naked as if it were his mother, and not a man with him...heh!"

The man's mind was wandering, Max decided.

"Another came out of the desert—a girl, dark-haired, like me."

"Ahhh...that one—!" The old man spat, his face wrinkling with disgust. "She came from no desert, that one. Too soft, too well-kept. Like you, you say? Might've been; she *was* a strange dark one. But not from the desert."

Max felt his heart sinking. Could there be others in the land who answered Fran's description? "How do you know, old one?" he asked harshly.

"Well, now...From what she said, for one thing. Never mentioned the desert; not at all. And we took her from one of the tribes to the east—and how would they have her, had she come from beyond the west, d'you suppose? And soft, like I said. Look at you. You, I can tell; you came from the desert, although you'd not been there too long. Hard, you are. The mark of the sun is on you, and that of hard living. That Fran girl, not a callus on her thumb." He nodded in agreement with himself.

Max brightened. "But her name—her name was Fran?"

"It was. A name as strange as the rest of her—not like any human I ever saw in this world."

"And where is she now?"

"Gone," old Kashrath said. "Gone to another world."

Tapers cast a flickering light in the low-ceilinged room. Their flames picked out details, here and there, leaving all else shrouded in shadow. Max was aware of the heavy, rough-hewn beams only inches over his head, slabs of stone set across them, bridging their gap and creating the door for the level above. He was aware too of the musty odor, muted by the smoky tapers but still persistent. Max shook himself. The damp lent a chill to his body that the temperature did not call for. Kashrath's basement workshop seemed almost a dungeon.

He stood, impassive, holding every outward show of emotion in check, while inwardly his thoughts seethed.

*So close...*He had been within a day of Fran, of his Fran. When all had seemed hopeless, his quest a fool's errand, hope had been breathed into his spirit again by word of Fran—the first he had heard of her in this world.

It had made sense, of course, and he had known from the first he'd heard of Rassanala's raiders that if he was to find Fran anywhere in these lowlands, it would be here. Everything gravitated here eventually—even he had.

And now—what had this old fool said?—she was gone again. "Gone to another world."

Kashrath stepped back, involuntarily, bumping back against a workbench and setting its glassware to tinkling as the dark man before him reacted to his words. The man's face had tightened, and Kashrath braced himself for a blow.

The blow did not come. Instead, Max asked only, "How? How did she do this?" And his voice carried a quiet chill.

"Ah," said the old man. "Come; I will show you.' And he did.

Leading the way back through a twisting way among the clutter, old Kashrath stopped at last before a strange object.

At first Max thought it was simply a door, a door into another of the rooms in this labyrinthine cellar. Then he saw that it stood apart from the wall; that it was indeed a door, set in its own frame, but standing several feet from the wall.

It looked out of place among the alchemical apparatus that cluttered this arcane workshop. Its design was wholly apart from that of its surroundings. The light here was dim, but it appeared to be made of a still-shiny alloy, a dusky silver in color, blue glints reflecting in places from the light of the tapers. The door itself was set on concealed hinges, and set on its front were what Max first mistakenly thought were ornamental pieces of scrollwork. Then he saw that they were a series of buttons. All but one were coated with damp and dust. That one was brighter. And it was depressed.

Kashrath leaned forward and seized the door's handle, and then threw it open. "Behold!" he said. In his attempt to be dramatic, he'd failed. His voice had cracked.

Max saw nothing. Then he realized that indeed he saw *nothing.* The way between the open portals was black. Too black.

Where the flickering light of the tapers should have shown him the rough stone wall beyond, he saw nothing.

"Observe," Kashrath said. He picked up a piece of glass tubing from the dusty bench nearby. He tossed it through the doorway.

The thin tube of glass winked once in the light, and then vanished.

Max peered around behind the doorway. The space between it and the wall was empty.

"Another world?" Max asked.

"Who can say? *Somewhere* else...that is all I know." The old man tittered. "It does well for the disposal of litter—far easier on an old man's bones than the carrying of heavy loads up the steps."

"And—and Fran went through that?"

"She did." The man spat again. "I'd told her of how I'd found it in the ruins of the old City Shanathor, and how I used it, and she became all excited. And then before I could stop her, she'd jumped through the thing herself. Heh...I've not told Rassanala yet, you can be sure of that. He—hey, what're you doing?"

Max looked once over his shoulder. "You needn't tell him about me, either," he said. And then he stepped through the portal.

Chapter 14

There was a moment of disorientation, of blackness. And in that split second Max felt a dizzying familiarity—a familiarity born of his first trip to this world.

Then he found himself in another room, and dust lay thick on every exposed surface.

Deep yellow sunlight poked its way through a window, but the window itself was so encrusted with grime that Max could see nothing through it but light and shadow.

The room reminded Max in a vague way of another room he had been in, but at first he could not place it. Then, as he sneezed, it came back to him. The ruins of Shanathor. Was he back in that dead city again?

He stared around him. The room had a long-stripped look to it; it was devoid of all furniture but the now-closed portal which stood near one wall. Max regarded the portal thoughtfully. Then he looked at the floor.

The dust was heavy and undisturbed on the floor in most places. But leading from the portal were tracks. Most of them were his tracks, leading from the portal to the window, and then turning to come to a stop where he now stood.

But another set of tracks led directly from the portal to a nearby door.

Max stood and examined them more closely. These were not neat tracks such as one might find in snow—rather they were scuffings, disturbances in the dry dust where someone had walked, kicking the dust into the air, from which it settled again.

But Max had learned much during his trek across the desert; it was obvious that the feet which had left these tracks were smaller than his own. *Fran's?*

In the corridor beyond, he found an open window.

The corridor floor was paved with faintly iridescent blocks irregular in shape. Overhead the ceiling panels glowed softly. The effect was the shadowless luminescence of an overcast day. There was no dust here, not even on the window sill. Max leaned on the thick sill and stared out over the city.

Tall, unbroken towers rose from neatly patterned streets. The buildings were of many colors, and some were softened by a mantle of green—an ivylike vine, Max surmised. Other buildings were terraced, plants growing down their sides in a fashion which reminded Max of half-remembered history lessons and the Hanging Gardens of Babylon.

The sun hung low in the west, and a little to the north of it was the glint of water.

Where was he?

He stared more closely down into the darkening canyons between the buildings. He was, he estimated, ten or more flights up. Below he thought he detected movement, people.

At first he'd he thought of the ruined Shanathor, but this city was not dead. *Where had old Kashrath's magic portal sent him?*

A sudden blow glanced off the side of his head, struck his shoulder, and drove him to his knees.

Still dressed in flowing robes, Max tripped as he tried to rise and whirl, and instead flung himself to one side in a crouch and faced his opponent.

The man was short—barely over five feet in height—and stocky. The man's hair was sandy, his skin weathered leather, his face dominated by a huge nose. The nose almost hid his eyes, buried in deep squints back on each side of it, and dwarfed his small mouth, now clamped shut and thin-lipped. His head was set low on his neck, giving Max the first impression that the man had no neck but that his head was a post set upon his shoulder and supporting only a nose.

Now he stood, wide-legged, a heavy-looking walking staff held across his chest in both hands, braced for Max's next move.

Max held himself still, still crouching low, coiling his muscles.

The other feinted to one side, then lashed out with the staff. It whipped the air over Max's suddenly ducked head with a heavy swiping sound.

Then Max launched himself forward, under the other's guard, before the staff could be brought to strike again. He rammed his shoulder into the stocky man's midsection, and both fell to the floor, Max on top.

But his opponent was no weakling; his torso was a wall of muscles, and Max had not even winded him. Now he pushed thick arms up and threw Max off him, whipping out from under and snapping again to his feet. Once again Max found himself waiting, crouching—and his only advantage was that the other had lost his stick.

Without taking his eyes off the man, Max sidled to his left and reached for the staff. As his hand closed on it, the sandy-haired man rushed him.

Max made as if to jump left again, and then went to the right, thrusting the staff out as he did so.

The wooden pole went between his attacker's legs, and the man tripped. The staff was wrenched from Max's hand, and then again he leapt on the other.

He knocked the man flat on his face, and then was braced on his back, one arm locked around his head, the other twisting the man's arm back. It was an impromptu hold, but effective. The man flailed with his free arm but could not reach Max. Then he tried to throw himself over, but Max tightened his hold and the man grunted with exertion and pain. Without relaxing his tensed muscles, the man tried to gasp a few words.

Max did not let up on him, but relaxed the hold on his throat a little. "What's that you say?" he asked.

"Give—" the man rasped, "I—give."

Warily, Max released the man. They climbed to their feet and regarded each other again, sizing each other up anew.

There was a flinty strength to the ugly little man, Max realized; a strength he'd not have known was there had he not fought the man. He looked like a small shopkeeper, and his homeliness was somehow a part of his nondescript appearance.

Suddenly the man's face burst into a grin. "Well done, stranger! It's been a long time since I've had an honest workout."

Max felt the tension drain away then, and knew at last that he'd won—he'd won a greater battle than that of muscles, and one he'd not more than sensed.

"I'm Max Quest," he said, and let his own features relax into a weary smile. "And it's been a very long day."

"Ah!" exclaimed the other. "And I am Hagendorf, too often known by my friends as Dorf. You will accompany me to my apartment for dinner." He thrust out his hand, and Max clasped it. The handshake was strong and firm, the shake of two men who had found each other's measure, and with it a strong respect.

"This is the city Zominor," Dork told his guest as they relaxed over a dinner of true culinary delight. Max found himself being served four different cuts of meat, endless varieties of crisp and cooked vegetables, and glasses of light, biting wine, all from an automated console by the dinner table. Periodically Dorf would finger a combination of buttons, an orifice in the console would open, and slim metal fingers would extend and place a new dish. Max was too tired and too hungry to maintain any great curiosity about the manner in which the food was served, however. A great lethargy had overtaken him, the aftermath of almost twenty-four hours of incredible strain and fatigue. He could barely keep his mind on what his host was telling him.

"We were the only continent not struck by the cataclysm, centuries ago," Dorf was saying. "The twin cities of Zominor and Azanor here still stand; we are the only ones left who still remember and preserve the ancient arts. The other great cities...Ialla, Vagar, Shorgot, Qanala, Shanathor, Tanakor, all the others...all fallen now; all dust."

"Shanathor—" Max said, the name catching his attention. "I have been there."

"Ah!" cried Dorf. "Have you indeed? Tell me of it."

Max passed his hand over his face and wished for a breath of cool, fresh air to clear his head. He felt as though he were in a near-stupor; the cumulative effects of his fatigue and the satiation of his hunger were hitting him hard now.

"Dead—as you said," Max said thickly. "Fallen ruins. The people avoid it."

"People! There are people up there, then?"

"Nomads—plains people. And raiders. Rassanala. A two-bit feudal empire. I came from there today."

"What?" The little man's eyes widened with surprise. "From the northern continent?"

"Where are we?" asked Max. "I mean, where on this world?"

The question puzzled the man, but he strove for an honest answer. "Why, this is the Zanorian continent...we are in the southern hemisphere...we—this is an island, cut off from the northern, southern, and eastern continents. That is why our civilization has survived...only we alone still maintain ships capable of sailing the open seas to the other continents."

"Ummm," Max said to himself, "And Shanathor? That's in the northern hemisphere?"

"Yes," Dorf replied. His face was puzzled, but then suddenly it lit with understanding. "Of course! I am a stupid old man! Of course; that's why I found you in that corridor! You came through the transmitter, didn't you?"

"Transmitter? You mean that portal that stands by itself in the deserted room?"

"Ah, yes! Yes, you did."

Max nodded. "Yes. A matter transmitter; I see. And the other one came from Shanathor. An old sham wizard has it in the basement of Rassanala's rat nest. He uses it to throw his refuse in. So...it brought me here...." Adrenalin brought him back to sharp awareness. "Fran! A girl preceded me through the—the transmitter. Yesterday. I saw her tracks on the floor in the dust. Where is she?"

A sad look passed over Dorf's face. "I'm sorry, Maxquest, but only one has preceded you through the transmitter in all my memory, and she is the Sorceress of Zominor."

He slept long and deep that night. It was at first a troubled sleep, for he felt a deep sense of guilt—he was so elusively close to Fran now, and yet the demands of his body were impossible to ignore. He'd tried to sort the events of the day into a logical sequence in his mind, but it was impossible. Where had this day begun? With the midnight raid upon Ishmight's camp? With his arrival, dehydrated and his body feeling almost flogged to death, in Rassanala's stockade? He had done too much—and too much had been done to him—in the short space of twenty-four hours. Now he lay in a soft bed, silken coverlets over his aching body, and his spirit and his body fought for dominance. His body won. He fell asleep.

When he awoke, sunlight poured in through the windows, and Max saw what he'd been too tired to recognize the night before: the whole side of his room was a wall of glass.

When he climbed from the bed he was amazed at the new energy that infused him. By rights he should be a mass of aches and pains. Yet he felt refreshed and eager to be up and about. The time in the desert had seasoned him, he realized; he must take care that soft living did not decondition him as easily.

He found a bathroom adjoining his bedroom, and in it a stall which appeared to be a shower. The oil he'd been rubbed with the previous day had mingled with his sweat and turned rancid, and he was eager to be clean of it.

The stall had no shower nozzle, however. He saw nothing but a round button. Gingerly, he pushed it.

There was a faint click, and then a humming sound. Then, suddenly, he was engulfed in a mist.

There were tiny sprays coming from each of the four corners of the stall, he saw, starting down within an inch of the floor, and extending up to about the height of his neck. The spray was so fine that it formed an almost solid mist which swirled about his body.

The mist was warm, but not hot. And it was not water. Later, Dorf explained the system of chemicals to him, and the way the refresher's electric eye gauged his height. But now he knew only that the mist tingled, not unlike an aftershave lotion, exciting his circulation, opening his pores, and somehow dissolving the days' accumulation of sweat, dirt, and oil from his body.

After some five minutes the mist disappeared, and a shower of clean warm water hit him, this time without skipping his face. After a moment of it the water stopped, and jets of warm air buffeted him, drying him. It was a marvelous way to bathe oneself, Max decided; luxurious and indeed almost erotic.

Dressed again, he investigated the wall of windows and found that each panel could be slid aside. And beyond was an open balcony. He stepped out onto it.

The balcony wall was waist-high and heavy. A creeper plant—an ivy of some sort—completely covered the wall, and stretched down below him as well as above. Max craned his head, but could not guess how much taller the bulding was. It appeared to be at least twice as tall as his floor.

The sun, white as ever, but hanging well north of the meridian, did not burn as cruelly as he'd remembered it. The ivy was a dark green, with hints of lighter green here and there, where new growth was appearing. Max pulled at one vine which had poked over the wall and was probing the inner wall of the balcony, and it was wiry and tough, little tendrils sprouting along its underside to somehow find purchase in the smooth, obsidianlike material of the wall. There was a strange odor in the air, and at first Max could not place it. Then he did—it was the smell of boxwoods: a heavy, almost spicy scent which somehow tickled his nostrils. It was the ivy.

A gentle breeze plucked at the sleeve of his robe, and then again, more insistently. The ivy rustled lightly. Overhead fleecy clouds moved lazily.

He was facing east, he judged. The sun was still well in the forenoon—perhaps at ten o'clock. The city stretched out for miles in every direction. There were many buildings as tall as his, but they were not crowded close together. Below there were smaller buildings, and the green of parks and lawns before each building. Trees, too, dotted the sides of nearby streets. As he watched, he saw a tiny vehicle crawl down the street below, then stop. Two ants climbed out.

To the south, jagged blue mountains climbed vividly up from the horizon, forming a solid wall as far as the eye could see. East, and northeast—and, yes, to the north too—beyond the rolling green of fields and woodlots, there was the distant shimmer of water, water which stretched in all directions to the horizon.

Zominor, a city which had once held many millions, now had a declining population of only some ten thousand.

Once this had been a great city, one of the population centers of the world of Qanar, but the cataclysm had ended that. The great cities had been scattered across the vast distance of the globe, linked at first by sea and land travel, and then by the ingenious matter transmitters. Many of the transmitters still existed, but they were no longer reliable, and few dared chance their use. The greater arts of science and magic had been all but forgotten, and although the citizens of the Continent Zanor still preserved the lesser arts necessary for the maintenance of their many machines and mechanical servants, here too the long-forgotten catastrophe had wreaked its subtle damage.

With the severance of the lines of communication with the mainland, and the fall of the mainland cities, the people of Zominor and its sister city, Azanor, had lapsed into quiet, sedentary lives, their needs tended to by machines, their pursuits genteelly degenerating arts. "New music is still written, and new paintings still painted. We still see many new plays, for a play can occupy the minds and bodies of many. But—none of these recent works do more than echo the masterpieces of the past. We are dying, too, as surely in our own slow way as did the people of the mainland continents," Dorf told him. "we are the last blurred and diminishing echoes of the race which once ruled this world."

Dorf had maps, and he explained the geography of Qanar. There were four major continents, the largest the eastern continent, which bulked as much land mass as the other three combined. Cut down its center by a vast and almost impenetrable mountain range, only the western lands had ever been thickly populated. Beyond the mountains, to the east, was the Arathdom, about which little was known. Once the city Ialla had existed, at the southern tip of the vast mountain range, and the people there had traded with the Arath, but even the trade was highly secretive.

There had been many great cities on the eastern continent, the five greatest among them Ulloro, Banarajan, Tanakor, Vagar ("The equatorial city; it was perched on the equator, between two branches of the Great Mountains, where the sea poked far inland. A strange place, that; and strange people, black as the surrounding desert was white. Some say they were the product of mixed blood—the Arath, and humans. I think it was only the sun that burned them black. But then the sun was not nearly so hot then as it is now; no man could survive in Vagar now."), and Ialla.

To the west, across the sea, were the northern and southern continents. The northern Max had some acquaintance with; the principle cities there had been Shanathor and Paraganat.

The southern continent lay below the northern, two strings of islands joining them and marking the two mountain ranges which ran north to south down both continents. The southern continent was actually two, now, for with the warming of the sun the ice caps had grown smaller and the sea level risen, and the sea had cut across the lowlands, cutting that continent in two. The two major cities were Qanala and Shorgot.

Zanor lay to the west of the southern continent and a little south. And to the west of these three continents lay only a vast ocean that covered almost half the world, until eventually one again reached the eastern reaches of the eastern continent and the Arathdom.

Max was fascinated by the maps Dorf showed him and he could not refrain from making parallels in his own mind between this world—Qanar—and his own, Earth. The positions were not exactly the same, but if one followed rough outlines, Zanor could be considered Australia—an Australia far closer to the tip of South America than to Asia. Then, imagine South America with two great mountain ranges, the western terminating only halfway down; the eastern running to the tip, and beyond it another piece of land one-third as big off the southeast coast. The northern continents compared loosely with North America. The western mountains were placed in the approximate position of the Rockies, with a great desert extending east to the range of mountains Max had crossed. But these mountains followed the general course of the Mississippi River and led down into the Gulf, to form a new Florida farther to the west, and then the chain of islands which led to the southern continent.

A land bridge connected the continent with what Max could not refrain from thinking of as Greenland; it was on this easternmost part of the continent that Paraganat was located. Max recalled Ishtarn's story of a land of perpetual snow, and began to understand it.

The eastern continent was least analogous. Imagine the British Isles solidly joined to Europe; a smaller Africa joined without interruption to a long and narrowed Asia, the foot of which dropped far south into a sort of boot which curved under Africa—and there one might see a loose approximation.

Max was deeply grateful for the chance to pore over these maps, for only now was he gaining any real idea of the nature of the world to which he'd come. It had already crossed his mind that he might grow old here, that whether or not he ever found Fran, they might never leave. Now at last he began to gain a grasp of the world he might be forced to adopt as his own.

There were the minor pleasures, as well. At last he could satisfy his curiosity about what lay to the west of the desert in which he'd found himself—and he was glad he had chosen the course to the east. He now felt certain that he would not have survived the much longer trek west—and of course he would never have found Fran's trail.

Chapter 15

An elevator took them to the street level, and a small, quietly humming three-wheeled car carried them through the nearly empty streets to the west.

This part of the city looked abandoned; it had a hollow, empty feel to it. "This was the business center, where world commerce was controlled," Dorf explained with a wave of his hand. "No use for it now." But the lawns were still kept up and the buildings had not fallen into decrepitude. It was more like a park—or a museum.

Then they turned from one wide avenue into another, and Max felt his breath halt. Before them, set in a square around which the avenue detoured, was a great black cube. It was featureless and perfectly regular. Looking at it alone, there was no way to judge its size.

Max stared around him, at the trees which lined the avenue, and the empty-faced buildings which climbed behind them. Then he looked back at the black cube.

It must be all of fifty stories high, he judged. It was monstrous.

They stopped in front of the vast building and climbed out of the small car. Max stared up the blank black walls.

Sunlight shone down through the leaves of the tree behind them, and dew glistened on the still-shadowed grass. The air smelled fresh and clean, with the hint of late spring in it.

The sunlight struck the building side cleanly, and without reflection. Max stared closer. The wall was black—totally black. Standing close to it like this, he could not encompass the wall's reach without turning his head. It towered over him, seemed to wrap black arms around him. It was impossibly close. Max resisted the urge to break and run.

"It reflects no light," Dorf said, his voice breaking the silence and shattering Max's mood. "None at all. It can have a frightening effect on one—you can't get any idea of distance when you're up this close to it."

Max nodded.

"Each section of wall," Dorf continued, "is a radiation-absorbing panel. This building absorbs radiation on every wavelength—it'll register 'black' on any detecting device. Of course, that's not why it was designed that way. The radiation is converted to energy. Among other things, this is the powerhouse for the City Zominor."

"Among other things—?"

"Yes. It is also the Hall of the Sorceress. And it is she you seek; is that not right?"

Max nodded again. His brain felt benumbed. "Yes—yes, I guess so."

The entrance was inconspicious, and once inside Max felt a strange subsonic throbbing through the soles of his feet. "Generators," Dorf explained without his asking. They followed many luminescent corridors, and rose Max knew not how far in an elevator. Finally, they were in an anteroom. And before them was a door. It was a simple, featureless door. Max had only to open it and walk through. His heart hammered.

Dorf settled himself in a chair. "I shall wait here," he said, and waved Max on toward the door.

He had no choice left. He opened the door.

"You aren't Fran," he said. He felt a sense of shock, of emptiness. He'd felt it as he'd approached the door—an impending loss, a loss of...what? Hope?

The woman who faced him stood tall in her shimmering black robes. Her figure was slender, lithe. Breasts jutted imperiously against the silken fabric and long black hair fell in smooth straight sheets down over her shoulders. She was beautiful. She was not Fran.

"Whom do you seek?" she asked.

Max turned away from her, bitterness clouding his thoughts. *Another dead end.* A remembered phrase came to him in Dorf's voice... *"The transmitters aren't reliable any more..."* Once again—he'd been cheated. Was fate toying with him? Or—the Others?

"A girl," he said. "She went into a transmitter. I followed her, and it brought me here."

"No one else has come through the transmitter but I myself," the Sorceress said. "You will not find her here."

"I know," Max said. Defeat lay heavy in his voice.

"Come here," the woman said. "I want to look at you."

Without thinking, Max obeyed.

Closer to her, he saw that she was shorter than he'd thought. And that her long black hair fell easily to her waist. She looked up at him out of deep blue eyes. He stared back at her, into her eyes. Color swirled and glinted in those deep pools, blue changing to gray, and then to green, and back to blue, always shifting.

"I sense about you a great *mana*," she said, "An—aura, shall I say?" Her eyes widened. "You are a great warlock, whose powers are now in bondage!"

Max was startled. Could she really be possessed of magical powers? He had laid the talk of magic he'd heard from the old Kashrath and Dorf to misunderstood science. But—this woman's description, if you granted the context of her metaphysical vocabulary, hit very close to the mark!

"I understand," she said, "because, you see, I too am not of this time."

"Are you from Earth, too?" Max asked.

"Earth? No," she said puzzled. "I have never heard of Earth. I come from the past."

She came from before the time of disaster, she told him. She had no idea how it happened, but apparently one of the transmitters malfunctioned. It threw her some three thousand years ahead in time. She had been astonished to find herself in an empty, dusty room; far more astonished, and frightened, to find the City Zominor all but deserted. She had made for the Hall of Science, hoping to find her answers there. And there the people had found her, and proclaimed her Sorceress.

"I have no magical powers, really," she said. "Or rather, in my time we did not regard them as magical. Now...I do not know. Here I am Sorceress, and I have indeed *become* Sorceress. I am given one of the Gifts—I can see something of another's thoughts. I was tested for them when I was younger—back in my own time. But they were too erratic; I could not rely on them. I trained as a scientist. Here even my intuition seems magnified, and it is given to me to know those whom I meet. When you add in my scientific training—" she laughed lightly— "the combination makes me a sorceress. They prize me highly."

"There is something not quite right about you," she told him.

"Something—I cannot explain it, but I sense it. You are not, umm, in phase, exactly."

She stood him on a small patch of shiny metal, between two upright metal posts. "Perhaps I can remedy that," she said.

She disappeared around the corner of a bulky cabinet and he heard strange noises—noises of switches being thrown, and the snapping of relays, the humming of power, and the vague crackling of metal elements heating and expanding.

He wondered what he was doing here, standing barefooted upon a metal plate, perhaps about to be electrocuted for all he knew. This woman—this Sorceress—made no sense to him; she'd as much as admitted that she knew little more than any trained technician of her day. What was this apparatus, and what did she hope to accomplish with it?

But he stood docilely on the metal plate, between the two posts. His will and his drive had departed from him. Despair all but inundated him. He had clung so long to the thin threads of hope, to the slim justification for his quest, that it had become his total *raison d'être,* and without it he was lost.

Since he had entered this world, he had been forced to fight for survival. He had been pitted against man and the elements. And he had won. He had fought his way ahead, each battle as he came to it, always clinging to than slender hope of finding Fran. He'd had little time to spend in introspection or the contemplation of the futility of his quests in the early days. Then, when—was it only yesterday?—he had actually heard word of Fran, it was the kindling of such fires of hope and gladness that he almost could not stand it—and he had been fearful, even then, that his new great hope might prove deceptive, a will-o'-the-wisp, and blink out of existence even as he laid his hands upon it.

Now it had. That Fran was still on this world—Qanar, they called it—he could no longer be sure. *That damned transmitter.* If it could bring one person into her future, it could as easily displace time or distance for another. Fran might be anywhere, anywhen. And there was no way he could comb the lands of a thousand times for her. The fires of hope had been quenched, killed.

The humming had been building until now the very air shook with it. He smelled the burnt smell of ozone, and his skin tingled with the electricity in the air. A faint memory came to him of another time, another place, and the smell of ozone blotting out that of fresh-mown grass.

It grew and grew, until the very air around him seemed almost to congeal. He stared around him, wide-eyed. *And then he*

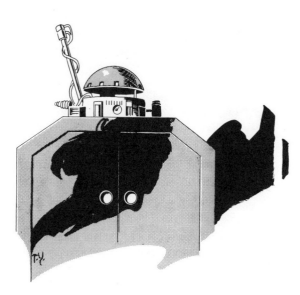

began to become aware.

A shell had formed around him, a strange and intridcate shell of energy. He sensed—saw—was aware—of its intertwined latticework. There was something he could not understand about it, about the way in which it seemed to...conflict...with the free and random energy in the room beyond.

Then he understood.

Carefully he drew the energy shell in, closer to him, until it fitted around him like a second skin—and then closer, until it *was* his skin.

Then he shut off the machine.

The air was suddenly empty, the room deafeningly silent. The Sorceress stared around the cabinet at him with wide eyes.

"The machine—" she said, "Did you—?"

A great weariness struck Max, like the blow of a hammer. He nodded. "Yes, I shut it off. It had done its work." He stepped down from the metal plate, and his feet found his shoes.

He probed out into the room, out into her.

And almost fainted.

He felt her strong arms helping him to his feet, and then he staggered into another room, and fell heavily upon a couch. The girl regarded him with worried eyes.

"You are still under a strange spell," she said.

Max shook his head, wearily, "No...Or, maybe yes. You could look at it that way. I understand it now."

It all went back to his original insight—that this world did not *exactly* correspond to his own. A did not equal A—But rather, A equalled A'. Realities were tangential in places, but did not completely correspond.

Qanar was not Earth. There were some fascinating parallels and similarities, but Qanar was not Earth. Nor was Qanar's universe Earth's universe. Again, subtle differences existed.

These subtle differences had stripped Max of his newfound powers—just as the Others might have known they would. Yet, even without most of his paranormal powers, Max was still not quite "in phase," as the Sorceress had put it, with this world. Perhaps that explained his extraordinary ability to absorb physical punishment.

The sorceress had made use of a machine which was a variant on the machines which powered the matter transmitters. The transmitters worked through a sort of local space-warp, bending space back upon itself so that one could move directly from one area into another. And in so doing, they approximated a moment removed from the reality of Qanar's universe.

With her machine, the Sorceress had created a local anomaly around Max, an anomaly of energies which allowed his own universe to co-exist in uneasy balance with the universe of Qanar. Max had drawn the envelope of energies in around himself, and fitted it to himself. And now his powers were restored.

But at a terrible price. For the energy shell which allowed him the use of his powers was itself no longer powered by the Sorceress's machine. It was powered by Max.

"I can feel it—the drain, the absorption," Max said. He pushed the bitterness from his voice. "As soon as I extend myself beyond myself, everything tends to cancel out."

"You should return to the transmitter," the Sorceress said.

"The transmitter? Why?"

"Didn't you say that once in transmission you would not be beset by this...this drain? And perhaps you could now—with your powers as a warlock restored—trace the one you seek."

"Not only my so-called powers—my brain is becoming enfeebled," Max said. He seized her by the arm and whirled her into a sudden embrace. "You're right, of course!" he said, laughing. He kissed her startled lips, and then released her.

Dorf looked up in wonder as Max burst through the door again and back into the anteroom. "You—you found her?" he asked.

"No—not yet," Max replied. "But I shall, old friend. I shall!"

"Maxquest," Dorf said as they descended in the elevator, "what has come over you?"

Max sobered. "Hope," he said. "Real, and genuine, hope. At last I can see a solution to my problems, an answer for all the questions."

Then they were in the dusty room again, and before them stood the enigmatic portal of the matter transmitter.

"Maxquest," Dorf said. "I sense a great change in you. You seem stronger, wiser, older. It seems impossible that we have known each other for such a short time. I—" He hesitated, his voice breaking. He thrust forward his hand. "Remember us," he said huskily.

Max took his hand, and for a moment held the clasp. Then he turned and stepped through the portal.

There was a sharp twist as he felt his axis rotated through reality, and in the same instant he slowed the passage of subjective time to a crawl.

He was floating in blackness—and yet, not blackness. Here there was an absence of everything, including blackness. He was caught in a moment between realities—a warp ouside the universe of Qanar.

He was filled with sharp realizations then, among them the knowledge of the four levels of the universe—matter, energy, space, and time. He was suspended, apart from all of these.

It was easier to understand now how the transmitters might misfunction, if their circuits malfunctioned, and they might act as inadvertent time machines. For their basic function depended upon the momentary transportation of their users outside of matter, energy, space, and yes—*time!*

Max wondered what the machines' users would have thought, had they been able to truly understand the principles upon which matter transmission had been based. Where was he now—*heaven?*

Where was God?

But he already knew.

He bent his mind to the task at hand.

He stood outside time. And, by exercising his mental faculties, he could probe this un-place, and find the traces of all who had ever passed unknowingly through it. *Traces?* There was no time here. Here they all came simultaneously, timelessly, out of "past" and "future" to be joined again in split seconds to reassuring reality.

Max saw it all, and understood. But he did not question. He saw too much, then, in that subjective eternity, and it stole his exuberance from him, reminding him only that his task remained.

There was Fran. A trail of ions? Fran—cutting a corner from that which had no corners...and disappearing back into—*there*.

Thin streaks of sunlight cut through the gloom. The place smelled dankly of earth and damp. Underfoot something crumbled, as Max stepped out of the long-disused portal.

There were windows, but they were heavily overgrown with vines, roots, creepers, and all manner of choking foliage. Max felt claustrophobic for a minute, and then oriented himself. Carefully, sparingly, he probed his surroundings.

He was in a ruined building, and to his right was a doorway. He felt his way to it, his feet shuffling over the uneven floor. Once they slid in something wet.

The doorway opened onto a hall, and at the end he could see a lighter oblong that marked the exit.

There was a faint chittering noise, and then a scrambling sound as something small and dark scurried past him, back into the gloom. Up ahead sunlight fell in patterns of white, yellow, gold, and green, and as he approached the opening fresh air momentarily pushed back the fetid odors of the underground.

Someone else had pushed through these vines, and the grass which grew in the dirt bank that half buried the doorway was bruised and mashed where someone else had climbed up and out.

How far ahead of him was she? It has been impossible to exercise control over the exact time of his re-entry into this world from the netherworld between portals—and the transmitter had still been affecting him. In all likelihood he had re-entered time at the moment where he had left it. And that made Fran—how long?—one, two days ahead of him here?

His brain ached. It seemed to him that as he pursued his tortuous quest his path became ever more twisted. He had understood so well, while he had stood in that moment outside time, but now the weight of conflicting realities passed down upon him, and his mind was again muddy, unclear.

Once he had pulled himself out of the hole, he found himself standing in a tiny forest clearing. Behind him were a series of hillocks, heavily overgrown with brush, trees twisting their way up from among them here and there. Before him was the heavy growth of forest, trees grown so large and so tall that he would have sworn he was in a forest primeval.

He looked behind himself again. Once these hillocks had been the base, the foundations of a mighty city. Now—? Now they were all but unrecognizable. What great cataclysm had been launched upon this world, some thousands of years earlier, to so destroy and bury its mighty civilization?

It was not easy to follow Fran's trail, for where the sunlight fell easily the grass and moss had restored itself and no longer left sign of her passing. But here and there, where the ground was soft enough to retain her imprint, or the grasses weak enough, and with the sparing, taxing, use of his paranormal perceptions, Max found her traces, and followed.

She had been wandering; that was plain to see. And then her path straightened, and a moment later Max could see the reason for himself.

Ahead, between the trees, he glimpsed a road.

Chapter 16

He stood at the edge of the road and stared down at its surface.

The road was actually a wide path or trail that cut through the forest, winding its way among the trees. In places it was rutted, and it was obvious that wheeled vehicles sometimes used it. But in other places, where the road widened and flattened out, the mark of narrow horseshoes was plain.

The road was of hard-packed earth, overgrown here and there by grass and moss, occasionally cresting flat rocks or stones. It had the look of age upon it, and Max was reminded of his childhoold explorations of a woodlot when he once spent a summer in the country. There he had found an inexplicable road, not unlike this one, but much more overgrown and long disused. It had begun out of nowhere and ended in the same way, a tangle of saplings barring its way. Midway down its length he had found the rusted chassis of an ancient automobile, resting now on the hubs of its wheels, long stripped of all but the solid block of rust which had once been its motor and the long forlorn shaft still topped by a wooden steering wheel. A bush grew where once the driver's seat had been.

Max had felt a strange and exhilarating sense of mystery on that long-forgotten summer afternoon, as though he had ventured into another world in which the modern days had been forgotten. He remembered that feeling now as he stood at the edge of this road, the sun stippling the ground before him, a soft warm breeze stirring the treetops, and somewhere in the distance a bird calling mournfully.

Which way had she gone?

There was no sign of her along the road in either direction. Sighing, he opened his second sight and began to reinspect the area.

He felt the thud of hooves before he heard them, and quickly he straightened to his feet, the blood rushing dizzily away from his wearied brain. There was no time for thought; he was too drained by his mental exertions to play more tricks with time. Quickly he threw himself into the underbrush at the side of the road and buried himself in the old, dried leaves beneath the bushes.

Four men rode by.

The men were tall, thick-chested, and sturdy, and they rode with an air of watchful alertness, long, rifle-shaped weapons loose in their hands, poised for use. Their faces were grim, their eyes narrowed.

All this Max saw, but he saw more. For the men were riding horned animals which reminded him of buck antelope or stags— proud, tawny beasts with great muscled shoulders and haunches, tapering to slender, graceful legs which picked their way surely and saunteringly along the road.

The men were bearded, the leader wearing a full, black beard, the other three red and brown-haired and wearing their beards trimmed, in one case to a goatee. They were dressed in tight-fitting leathers, tunics belted outside their pants. They had the look to them of forest men, and Max wondered who they represented, and what they might mean to him should he encounter them again.

He knew what to do, however. His mental probe had been completed. Fran had been picked up by passersby, and their path led in the same direction as that of this quartet. He would follow.

He made good time as he strode along the road, for his regenerative powers were standing him in good stead. The use of his paranormal abilities could drain him as surely as a battery might be drained, but restraint from their use quickly recharged him.

It was afternoon, he realized, as the sun dropped steadily behind him. The great trees shaded him well from its direct rays, but he could still keep track of its passing.

As the afternoon wore on, small flying insects began to follow him, buzzing about his head and darting at his eyes, nose, ears, and mouth, so that he took to swatting at them in a rhythm with his walking. He became grateful for the loose flowing robes which he still wore; they protected most of his body from the wearisome creatures. There was another reason as well: his robes

135

were in tones of green, and they blended well with the dappled aquamarine light of the forest.

After a time he came to a hollow where the four riders had stopped briefly before him. Their mounts had grazed the grass here and left droppings, and Max found the discarded remnants of a meal. The sight of them reminded him of his hunger, for he had not eaten since breakfast with Hagendorf. He knew he must be in another part of the world now, since it had still been only late morning when he had said goodbye to Dorf, and by rights it should be far earlier here than it was. But whether it was the psychological effect of the gathering dusk, or simply the product of many miles of walking and the jolts his nervous system had received during the day, Max was hungry. And hungry for a full meal.

He found berries on a nearby low-hanging bush, and ate several handfuls, but it was not enough.

He let his mind go blank and sent out little chittering thoughts instead; warm thoughts, friendly thoughts, hospitable thoughts. It was dishonest, perhaps, but all baited traps are dishonest.

It was not long before a small furry creature scratched its way down a nearby tree trunk and began to sniff its way around Max.

It made a sideways sort of scrambling, darting forward to lift its quivering nose, and then half leaping to one side and back, to dart forward again, its actions transcribing a circle around Max.

Max waited as long as he could, and then struck.

The jolt of energy stunned them both, but Max was first to pull himself up and throw himself forward upon the other. The small creature gave a spasmodic kick, and then lay still.

The light in the forest was dim when Max, much refreshed, pushed on.

The night was balmy, and Max followed the road until he estimated it was nearly midnight. Much of the time his way was lit by silvery moonlight, and the forest was a place of hushed enchantment.

Once Max thought he heard a padding sound beside him, and without thinking he spoke aloud to his wolf—only to find the road behind him empty.

In many ways he felt as he had those nights he climbed the mountains; there was the exhilarating knowledge that he was approaching his goal—then simply a greener land beyond the mountains, and now the surety that he would indeed find Fran.

There was something in him that held this night in a last

clinging embrace, too, for his foreknowledge, gleaned between the transmitter portals and now dimmed but still lurking, warned him that he would not know many more such nights on this world. And suddenly his every experience here was very precious to him.

He drank in the smells, fresh and rich—leaf mold, late-blooming flowers, the coming crispness of impending autumn—while his eyes encompassed the rich tapesty of mottled shades, grays with hints of greens and browns, and startled silver. Light breezes rustled the leaves overhead and plucked at his garments. If insects still swarmed at this hour, the breezes had blown them from him. He breathed deeply of the rich air and strode on. He did not stop until the larger moon had set and the forest had grown into a dark leafy hollow.

He awoke to see another furry tree-creature digging in the turf with its forepaws only a yard from his outstretched hand. He watched its industry for a long moment, and felt a pang of sharp regret when he felled it. But he did not feel wrong; he was attuned with nature, here in this great and womblike forest, and this was nature's way, each creature's existence partaking in another's existence. Only man, it occurred to Max, had ever attempted to break out of that cycle. And for what? To leave behind the mortality of the foraging for existence and interdependence with nature for the immorality of preying upon one's own kind, for wanton and heedless destruction of anything and everything, declaring complete independence of that which had birthed him. Max felt at that moment curiously remote from the species from which he was descended.

The sun was still low in the east when Max began again his trek along the road. He had no idea how much farther he would need to travel, but he felt within him a serene confidence. He *would* find Fran; he *would* return with her to Earth.

Less than an hour after he had set out, he came upon the site of the overnight camp of the four riders. Embers still smoked from an earthern pit where a fire had been laid, and the odors of man and beast were heavy still in the forest glade. Max lifted his head in an unconscious gesture and sniffed the air.

They could not be many minutes ahead; he must have nearly caught up with them during his nocturnal travels. He would have to be careful now until they pulled ahead again.

But they had no chance. He came upon them scant minutes later.

The forest had been thinning, and the sun struck more directly through the leaves and branches. Max was sweating lightly when the road curved, topped a rise, and then opened upon a meadow.

The dew was still heavy and glistening upon the meadow grass, the sun still low over the tops of the trees on the other side of the open area, but the meadow glistened with more than dew.

For Max at first the scene made no sense—and then it did, as he resolved the whirling figures into individuals and began to understand.

Hoarse shouts and angry epithets rose from the meadow glen, and horned beasts snorted and sometimes screamed. There were ten figures mounted, dashing and wheeling about. Only two were of those who'd ridden so carefully past Max the day before. The other two— One lay only yards away, his body only partly concealed by the heavy meadow grass, his blood staining it a bright and improbable red. The other one lay half under his dead mount near the center of the melee.

The remaining two had broadswords in their hands and were parrying and slashing against their attackers. It was easy to read the circumstances of this battle—the eight others had ambushed and set upon the four as they'd entered the meadow, and had scored their first victim almost immediately.

But *why*? Whose battle was this—and for what stakes? Max eased himself to the ground at the base of a large tree and cast his mind out, onto the meadow, into the battlefield.

It was an exhausting task. He had to deal with ten minds, and the task of sorting them into component bodies was difficult. It stunned him, too, to discover that distance had a considerable effect upon his abilities. It was like being in grade school again, confronted with a difficult problem in arithmetic. Over and over again he had to work the problems, checking and rechecking to be sure of his answers, his mind slowing and stumbling as he progressed.

But finally he had the answers. His head was in a swirl, and when he tried to stand he found he could not. Dazed, he crawled for the nearby fallen body.

The four who'd ridden out of the forest were all minor nobles of the area, pledged to the Duke of Qar. The political situation was impossible to discern—Max had only been able to pluck the thoughts off their minds' surfaces—but apparently the most recent Duke of Qar was bringing civilization back upon this land.

The attackers were outlaws, part of a band which preyed upon travelers on the road and harrassed the Duke. They'd stalked the Duke's men since early morning, and laid in wait for them here where they could be reasonably sure none of their quarry might escape. Max realized that he had been fortunate in escaping their notice himself.

By the dead man's side he found one of the strange rifle-like weapons he'd seen them carrying the day before. Up close it was was less impressive, and Max puzzled over its operation for a long moment before daring again to use his second sight to plumb its mysteries.

The weapon was constructed like a long barrel, some two inches in diameter and two feet long, with a thinner barrel protruding from one end for another two feet and a stock fastened to the other end. There were no sights. A fancy trigger guard resolved itself into a lever-mechanism that sank into the stock and ran its length when pressed out of sight.

It was a unique modification of the crossbow. Instead of a bow, or leaf spring, it used a heavy coiled spring, in the larger barrel, of the same power. By pulling the trigger guard out and levering it back, Max could cock the weapon. The leverage was efficient and easy, and even in his enervated state Max did not find it difficult.

He had to roll the dead man over to free his quiver of bolts. Then he dropped a bolt down the barrel, raised the weapon, and sighted.

The battle had moved his way, but no one was yet aware of his presence. Carefully he sighted on one of the outlaws' mounts—he needed a broad target to sight in on, and he did not wish to waste his shots.

The bolt pierced the animal in the front shoulder, and with a scream it dropped, throwing its rider. One of the Duke's men swung his sword toward the fallen man, but it was unnecessary. His neck was broken. Wheeling, the noble swung back to face another outlaw.

Max worked carefully and systematically, making every shot count. He was still weak and unable to stand, but he propped himself over the dead man's back and methodically cocked, loaded, and shot, over and over until suddenly—

The meadow was all but empty. Two horned mounts stood, heads down, grazing the grass with total unconcern. Nearby another kicked convulsively at the turf and attempted to rise. The kicks grew weaker, and then it began tossing its head wildly and digging with its horned antlers, tossing clods of grass into the air about it. Then it was still.

The meadow was dotted with other fallen beasts and men. Max counted six of the once-proud horned animals dead or dying.

One man remained mounted; the black-bearded noble who'd

led the quartet of riders past him yesterday.

Max pulled himself shakily to his feet. He held the cocked and loaded weapon loosely in his hands.

The rider approached him and nodded. "I thank you, stranger," he said. "It appears I owe you my life."

"We got them all, did we?" Max asked.

"No. Two cut and ran." The man's words were blurred and his head was drooping. Suddenly he seemed to fall into a slouch, and then he was tumbling from his mount.

Max dropped the weapon and jumped forward to catch him.

The man was wounded; his chest on his left side had been laid bare below the shoulder to the ribs. He had lost a great deal of blood, but it had run down inside his leather clothing and little of it had shown.

Max carefully straightened the man out and cut loose his tunic. He was startled to notice that the man did not wear true trousers, but rather a breechclout and leggings, after the manner of the western American Indian.

He found water in a bladderlike bag on the man's mount, and with it he cleansed and washed the wound as best he could. Then, tearing a long strip from his robes, he bound the flap of skin back over the wound and tied it into a tight harness that looped over the other's shoulder and would not easily work loose.

When he had stopped the flow of blood and attended to as much as he could physically, he let himself relax beside the man in the soft grass. Then he extended his mind into the other's body, working his way through it, dealing with the tetanus germs left in the wound by a rusty sword and now circulating through the blood system, stimulating the bone marrow to produce more blood cells, and knitting cells in the wound back together to help bind it and speed its healing.

He was close to unconscious when he had finished.

CHAPTER SEVENTEEN

The sun beat hot against his brow, and Max returned to alertness to find himself consumed by a great thirst. He found the water bag nearby, and the water, throught the miracle of evaporation, was still cool on his throat.

"Water—please?" The wounded man was conscious and pushing himself up with his right arm. Max knelt and held the mouth of the water bag to the man's lips.

"How do you feel?" Max asked.

The man felt under his left arm, and then carefully flexed the arm. A look of surprised wonder came over his face. "Why—how strange! I feel almost as though I were healed."

"How's your strength? Think you can ride?"

The man lifted a hand, and Max helped him to his feet. He teetered for a moment, then found his balance. "I'll manage," he said.

"What're the chances of those two who escaped coming back with help?" Max asked.

The man thought for a moment. "Not good. Not good for us, I mean."

Max gingerly approached one of the grazing animals. It did not shy off from him, and he took its reins and led it back to where the other's mount stood.

"I'm Max Quest," he said. "And you?"

"Elron—at your service," replied the other. He bowed, his face paling from the effort.

"Let's skip the fancy footwork and get out of here," Max said tersely. He watched Elron climb his mount. It was very like mounting a horse, he decided. Checking the animal's saddle bags to make sure they were loaded, he swung up and found himself in a broad saddle, his robes bunched high on his bare thighs.

They rode across the meadow and into the forest opposite, and they followed the road through that forest for the whole long day. There was little opportunity for talking. Max found his animal's jouncing gait jarred the breath from him whenever he tried to speak, and Elron was obviously holding onto what strength he had remaining for the ordeal.

That night, while they camped, Max questioned Elron.

The man knew nothing of Fran, but a caravan had preceded his party along the road by a couple of days. If, as Max seemed to think, she had been picked up, it would have been by the caravan.

The road ran from the mountains in the west and the ruined city of Ullore beyond them, past the vanished city of Tanakor, to the new city Qar, located on the banks of the river Qar. It was said that the road paralleled an ancient road, but if so all traces of the earlier road had vanished except for an unusually accessible gap through the mountains.

The city Qar had been built near where the river Qar was joined by its eastern tributary, and marked the first new city built in this part of the world in thousands of years. The present Duke of Qar was expanding his sphere of influence to the west, and had sent Elron and his three fellow officers west beyond the mountains to survey the situation and bid the wandering people there to join his state of Qar. The caravan was one of several which would be bringing travelers to the city Qar.

But outlaws ranged along the road to Qar, raiding caravans and preying upon travelers. They resented the spread of the Duke's power—and now they would no doubt feel his wrath for their attack upon his men.

The saddle bags held ample food, and the two ate well enough. Elron, having answered Max's questions at length, now was curious about Max. Why did he wear those strange green robes? Where had he come from, to appear at that meadow site so fortuitously?

Max parried most of his questions, saying only, "I am a stranger here, seeking a woman whom I have followed a long way." But to Elfon's insistent questions, he added that he had come from another part of the world, by means which Elron could only conceive to be magic.

"My wound—you used magic on that as well, did you not?"

Max sighed. "Call it that, if you wish."

And Elron did. It was clear he had made up his mind that

Max was a person of great magical abilities.

They rode out of the forest the following afternoon, and found themselves at the sandy banks of a broad river.

Beyond the river rose the sheer walls of a city. In a curious way it reminded Max of Rassanala's fortress city, but the gates to this city lay open, and he could see people moving about freely, and beyond the city open fields dotted with grazing animals and crops.

Nearby a great woven cable was fastened to a stout old tree which grew lower on the bank than most. Elron gave a hail, and Max followed the cable with his eyes to the far shore, where a ferryman was starting to pole his flat-bottomed craft out across the water.

Twenty minutes later they were riding through the open gates and into the colorful city of Qar.

Ranked along the wide roadway that led toward the center of the town were the shops and bazaars, merchants crying and hawking their wares—the merchandise running the full gamut from vegetables and food to leather goods, swords, all manner of hardwares, fabrics, and—Max was astonished to note—even women. The latter sat under awnings, dressed in fine fabrics but with their breasts bared and strategically placed slits in their skirts which were hidden among the folds until they moved. A man would approach one, silver would be exchanged, and the two would then disappear into the house behind them.

There was a frank and open bawdiness to this city Qar, and Max decided that he liked it. It was the vulgarity of youth, brashness combined with vigor, and Max sensed a great opening, growth, and development for these people. In a way he envied them.

But the afternoon was to be a disappointing one.

They found the remnants of the caravan first, Elron suddenly reining his horned steed to a halt and calling out to a weary-looking man in bloodstained leathers.

"Ho, Galt! You look as though you've seen trouble!"

Galt looked up. "Ah Elron," he said. He spat into the dust at his feet. "We should've had you and your fellows riding with us. Damned raiders came out of the trees on us; took most of our goods and most of our women. And the clucks I had with me stood by, their jaws agape!"

Elron commiserated and reported the fate of his own party.

"Damned outlaws," said Galt, spitting again. "It'll be the

143

Duke you're to see, eh? And maybe *he'll* do something about them hell-spawn!"

Max had sat silent through this exchange. A great weariness of spirit had descended upon him. Was there to be no end to this great farce? It was the worse because he knew now of his eventual success, and this continual drawing out served only as an annoyance.

"Did you pick a young woman up along your way?" Max asked. "In the forest?"

"That one," Galt said. "A spy for the outlaws, I'm thinking. Had we not been stopped for her, they'd not taken us so completely unawares." His eyes narrowed. "And what would you know of her, stranger?"

Elron intervened. "This is Max Quest," he said. (Max felt a profound sense of shock in hearing his name pronounced correctly, as two words, for the first time on this world.) "I owe him my life, and I'll hear no ill of him. He seeks the girl. The outlaws have her, you say?"

Galt nodded. "A strange one, she," he said doubtfully. He squinted again at Max in his incongruous green robes, spat a final time in the dust, and then turned his back on them.

They rode up the street for a time in silence. Finally Elron spoke. "All his worldly goods, his three wives, his family—he lost them all. He is bitter."

Max never got to meet the Duke. Elron had reported to his superior, and it was planned for them to have an audience with the Duke the following afternoon. But Max had had enough of waiting.

"Tomorrow morning," he told Elron, "I am leaving. I'll take the animal I've been riding."

"Where are you going?"

"You know where I'm going. I'm going hunting for those outlaws, and when I find them, I'm going to find my woman. I'm fed up with waiting."

Elron nodded slowly, and followed Max out to the street.

Dusk was falling, and torches had been lit along the streets. If anything, there were more people thronging along the way now than earlier. "Do they ever sleep?" Max asked Elron, "—or eat?"

A herdman drove his flock of goats up the street then, and passersby leaped or were forced, cursing, out of their way. One burly man leapt back into Max. His foot came down hard on Max's instep.

Max grunted, and the big man whirled, glaring angrily at the man who had the temerity to stand where he happened to be leaping.

"You—!" the man growled. "Whaddya think you're doin' there?"

"Minding my own business—up to now," Max replied.

The other raised his arm and threatened Max with the back of his fist. "Watch yourself!"

Max stepped back into the stable doorway, and the big man, sensing an easy victim, advanced. "Whaddya wear that crap for?" he asked, reaching out and fingering Max's robes. The robes were much tattered and soiled, and he had hoped to replace them with more suitable clothing, but he didn't care for the big man's tone.

"Hey—you one of those boys think they're girls, haw?"

Max chopped down quickly with the edge of his hand, catching the man's wrist and knocking his hand from its grip on the robes.

The man stepped back, holding his wrist with his other hand. His eyes squeezed nearly shut, and the expression on his face had become vicious.

"Max," said Elron behind him, grasping his arm, "let me handle this."

"No," said Max, pulling loose.

The big man was cursing now in a steady stream, and his curses concerned Max's ancestry, present condition, and his likelihood of surviving into the future.

"Watch your tongue, fellow," Max said. Then he reached out his hand, and extended his index finger at the man's mouth.

A single tongue of flame leapt from his fingertip and struck the man in his open mouth. The man gave a startled scream, clapped his hand over his mouth, gave Max one wide-eyed stare, and then turned and ran.

Max leaned against the doorway for a moment, regaining his strength.

"What did you do to him?" Elron asked.

"He was using pretty fiery language, so I gave him the taste of it," Max replied with grim humor. "That was more effective than a good thrashing for him."

They rode out of town soon after dawn. Max had tried to dissuade Elron from joining him, but the bearded man was adamant. "You saved my life, and I have pledged my life to your service."

"But the Duke—"

"He will hear all I could tell him in any case. It is better for me to ride with you and hope I can avenge my comrades." Elron, convinced Max was a great warlock, had hitched his own career to Max's destiny.

It was a full day's ride before they reached the fringes of outlaw territory. That night Max laid himself down after eating and pretended to fall asleep. While his body relaxed in a near coma, he sent his spirit out, roving, seeking sign of the outlaws.

He found nothing.

The following morning Max, looking haggard and still weary, led the way once more, following the quiet trail through the awakening forest.

They encountered the meadow that afternoon. It was as bare as if no man had ever seen it, only the beaten tracks of the road belying human presence. The outlaws had stripped the meadow of every sign of their attack. It was, Elron said, typical of them; there would be nothing to alert future travelers should they use this as a place of ambush again.

Max searched the edges of the meadow carefully, and by the north edge he found what he was seeking: a faint and well-disguised trail. They turned upon it and began threading their way as silently as possible between the twisted trees and up and down over occasional outcroppings of rock. This was not a smooth road for wagons and wheeled vehicles—this was a trail to be ridden in secret, and known by few. They maintained a wary alertness now, Max risking an occasional mind probe ahead every half hour or so.

Yet it was not until the golden rays of the sun slanted sharply through the leaves from the west that he found that which he sought.

He lifted his hand and reined to a halt. Elron drew abreast of him and stopped. "They are ahead, no more than a quarter mile," Max whispered.

"Where?" asked Elron. "I see nothing."

"I see them only in my mind," Max said. "In the trees. They have built a holding in the branches of the trees. In broad daylight we might ride directly underneath and miss them."

"But they would not miss us," Elron grunted.

"No," Max agreed. "They would not."

They ate a cold meal and made camp, off the trail in a well-protected hollow, until night fell. Then they led their mounts carefully and quietly along the trail until they were as close as Max dared bring them.

The outlaw holding was a series of rude buildings set high in the branches of the trees, ramps and rope bridges linking building to building and tree to tree. The total complex, Max estimated, covered five of the giant trees and housed perhaps forty outlaws. Robin Hood's band, he mused, never had it like this.

There were coiled rope ladders which could be lowered from the trees, but only two were down, and each was guarded. He sent his mind questing into the branches....

He found Fran in the hut of the outlaws' leader, tied and bound upon his bed. Her mind seethed with anger, and the anger communicated to his own.

"We act *now*," he said softly, but urgently, to Elron. "Let nothing surprise you. Unsheath your sword and have it ready to defend us."

Then he levitated the two of them up into the air. The startled Elron strangled a squawk of surprise and fear, and then they were among the leafy branches of the tree and standing on a wide limb near the trunk. Ahead of them was a crude hut.

Max steadied himself with an iron effort and strode out along the branch. He whipped aside the leather drape that covered the doorway and entered a foul-smelling, ill-lit room.

Fran was spreadeagled upon the bed, her body glistening with sweat and quite naked. A thin, wiry-bodied man with balding gray hair was standing over her. He too was naked, his body in an obvious state of arousal. He held Fran's hair with one hand, and it was plain to see what he was up to.

The man was so intent upon his actions that he did not become aware of the intruders until both were in the small room. At first he did not turn his head, but snarled, "Get out! I'm busy!"

Fran's eyes widened as she recognized Max and saw him seize Elron's proffered sword. Then Max brought the weapon down and with one cleaving blow sliced the outlaw chieftain shoulder to gut.

Somehow the man had breath for one shrill scream before he died.

"That did it!" Max said. He passed the sword back to Elron. "Hold the door," he said. He pulled a knife from his belt and cut Fran loose. Then he shucked off his outer robes and put them over her.

"Max, Max, Max," Fran sobbed, clutching at him with shocked relief. "Oh, Max—*how did you get here?*"

The hut began to shake, and overhead there were thuds as men dropped down from above. Suddenly a trap door swung open in the ceiling, and a man thrust his head down and through. Max promptly pulled his arm free of Fran and swung the knife still in his hand. It ripped the outlaw's throat, and the man's head and shoulders tumbled through the opening, hanging head down.

"We've got to get out of here!" Elron shouted. "They're swarming all over the damned trees!"

"Fran!" Max said. The girl was still in a state of shock. He slapped her lightly. "*Fran.*" Her eyes focussed on him. "Stick with Elron." He pointed. "I'm going to do my trick."

Quickly he pulled the body of the dead outlaw down through the trapdoor. Then he lunged up through it.

As he emerged, he called upon all his strength for this night, and then he set himself afire.

This time he exercised a finer control; he did not let the flames burn himself or his clothes. Instead he was cloaked with a halo of flames—flames which *burned*.

He stalked out onto the roof of the hut, each step leaving the crudely hewn boards smoldering, each step driving the outlaws already massed upon the roof farther back.

He extended one fiery arm, and the flames scorched the face of one man who was too slow. He advanced, and they retreated. It was a small rooftop. Each man faced the choice: burn to death or leap to his death.

Not one faced up to the flaming apparition on the rooftop.

Chapter 18

They made camp that night after a long, hard ride, not stopping until the larger moon had again set and they had put much distance between them and the outlaw tree-holding.

Even then they were cautious and lit no fires. It was a warm night in any case, and Elron discreetly laid his bedroll some distance from Max and Fran.

Max held Fran in his arms for a long time, talking to her, telling her the story of his long quest and the far places he had seen. It felt strange to hold her here with him now, like this, for it was as though the eventuality of seeing her again had always been a dream—a goal that extended beyond the possible and immediate and into the improbable future that a man only hopes for in a distant way and never really expects to find.

In his mind, Max had made a division between his two lives—here and on distant, improbable Earth. Fran belonged to Earth, and it was hard to think of himself as the Max who had also belonged there. He was Max Quest, desert-forager, nomad-guest, warrior, even warlock. Where was the Max Quest who drove a taxicab and lived in a furnished apartment on the West Side?

Now, shatteringly, the two halves had been rejoined; he had found Fran.

"Almost—I don't want to go back," she said. "It's as though I was never really alive before. I was a terrified little flower back there—and you watered me daily with small kindnesses. But I was so very fragile, so timid and afraid. Now...it's as though if I go back there, I'll return to being who I was—what I was."

She told him of her adventures. "They haven't been very

149

pleasant, or very romantic," she said. "I've gone tired and hungry to bed more nights than I haven't. I've been raped a number of times—and I've grown the emotional calluses. Like the old Chinese saying: 'When rape is inevitable, relax and enjoy it.' Some of them weren't so bad. Back when I was living with the goatherders, and every night I was given to another man in the hopes that somewhere along the line I'd become pregnant and introduce a new strain into their tribe. Those men were gentle. They smelled, but they were gentle with me."

"I first heard word of you in Rassanala's fortress," Max said.

Fran tensed for a moment and then relaxed. "They were the worst. Degenerates, the lot of them. Very refined. Nothing crude—like that old man in the tree hut—but very cruel, very nasty. When that old medicine man showed me where he threw his garbage, I figured I couldn't be treated any worse, and I jumped into—through—it." She stirred in his arms. "We've changed, haven't we, Max? We've grown up—grown older."

He stroked her gently. "It's been a hardening experience, Fran. I hope we can both profit by it."

"Do we have to go back? This is a huge world, and the places you've described...we could live in that city you were in—Zominor."

"No," Max said quietly. "We can't. We must go back. We must confront the Others. I have faced the sowers of destruction here, but they are only men, and they are not the foes I seek. I must deal with the ones who sent us here."

For a long time they simply lay together, quietly, sharing his bedroll as earlier they had shared his steed, and then as his strength gradually returned to him he began to caress her, unfastening the thin robes he'd thrown around her, freeing her of their constriction. And she in turn began unloosing his remaining robes, while their mouths found each other in long, sultry kisses.

This union there that night had a quality to it—a tempestuousness, an exultation—which they had never known together before, and it lasted for a long time...for Max knew, if Fran only sensed it, that somehow this was a moment too precious to waste.

That afternoon they came upon the buried ruins of the long dead city Tanakor. Carefully they retraced their path back in among the hillocks, until at last they stood before the gaping, weed-choked hole into the ground.

"We must leave you now," Max told Elron. The bearded man nodded sadly. His soft gaze took in the proud and happy faces of the couple who stood before him, and he nodded again in

"We must leave you now," Max told Elron.

acquiescence.

Fran held out her hand. "Thank you, Elron," she said. "We both thank you."

"You are returning to another world," Elron said.

"Yes," replied Max. "As you must know, this is not our world. It is a fair world—an old world being reborn. I could learn to love this world, if I remained here...and, indeed,"—he gave Fran an indulgent smile—"I wish I could. But our battle is not yet over. We have yet to face our final foes."

Max jumped through the hole and lifted his arms to Fran and swung her down beside him; then both disappeared in the darkness. Elron stood quietly on the turf for many long moments, his face in thoughful repose. Then suddenly he smacked his fist into his hand and dropped down into the hole.

He found himself in a long bare hallway which ran back into the gloom. Sunlight penetrated only a short way. But ahead he could see an opening off to the right, and he felt his way cautiously with his feet until he reached it and looked in.

Plants had not entirely closed the higher windows of the chamber; streaks of muted sunlight probed into the room. It was a strange room, half filled with clutter.

Near the windows the room was empty, the floor wind-blown and rain-washed with soil and silt. But at the other end of the room....

The floor was strewn with litter: pieces of fractured glass tubing, geegaws of tarnished metals that still caught an occasional mote of light, and even what looked like the former contents of a chamber pot.

Elron picked his way carefully to that side of the room and stood at last before a metal door. On the door was a filigreed pattern of round and square buttons, and if he'd had enough light he might have discovered archaic markings upon each button.

He touched the metal of the door, and a faint tingle ran along his fingertips. He stared at the door a long time. Then, as the light in the room began to wane he turned away at last and made his way for the outer door.

They hung in no-space for no-time.

Here Max was freed of the crippling inertia to which he'd been subjected on Qanar—here he was free to let his mind grow and expand.

They were between portals. But this time they would not return through the matter transmitter to Qanar.

They were removed from the universe Qanar. And Max had

foreseen this—had seen their emergence from Qanar together—when he had last passed between portals. For no time passed here, and all was—to someone who still viewed time subjectively, and could not think beyond temporal confines—*now*, an eternal present with duration. Max could not discipline his mind to fully accept the state of this existence; he could intellectually grasp the broad concepts, and he could observe some of the manifestations—if they could be called that—but he could not give himself wholly to function in this...environment. Properly speaking, he was an alien, trespassing here. He was a two-dimensional figure stepped off its sheet of paper—and now in a no-dimensional world.

Yet, because this was a no-place, of no-time, trespassers coexisted here, and all *were*, here.

But if this no-place was outside all universes, and outside Qanar's, it was also outside Earth's; and equally important, Earth should be as accessible as Qanar. There being no distance here, Earth could be—must be—as "close."

But—*where?* How did one find it?

Here, between space and time, he coexisted with Fran. In another sense, he *was* Fran, and she him—and it was thus that he sensed an indefinable spark that seemed to communicate between her here and—*Earth?*

But there was no analgous spark of his own.

Then he understood. It was the Others' final treachery.

They had not brought their bodies with them to the world of Qanar; he'd known that. Their bodies had lain on a couch in the mirror-image of the apartment-offices of Edwards & Archer. Yet they had identical bodies on Qanar. And there was a thin thread connecting the two—the spark he'd discovered.

But the Others had taken no chance on his returning to Earth victorious. They had given him nothing to come back to. They had destroyed his helpless husk of a body. He could not bring his Qanar body with him, for it was a part of the reality of Qanar's universe. It would not fit into Earth's reality.

Could he return to Earth without a body? He tried—and felt a splitting sensation. *He was losing Fran.*

No, you won't, came her thought.

I can't return without a body. If I try, your thetan starts to return to your body, leaving me here—trapped in limbo.

Return with me—to my body.

Coexist—share Fran's body with her? Max gave the idea thought—aware as he did so that he was thinking Fran's thoughts as well as his own.

153

Two of us—
—Just we two...!
Could we do it? The coordination—
—Would be easy, dearest.
The most intimate form of marriage...
—Till death do us part.
But without some of the usual advantages.

And in the back of his mind, he was aware of something else. This partnership would not be of that long a duration. But he kept that thought and its implications to himself.

Fran, I want you to know this: I love you.
I know, dearest.

They found themselves in Fran's body. It was lying in a bed, eyes closed, muscles relaxed, respiration slow—"asleep."

Best you handle the, umm, feminine movements—and let me direct the overall policy, as it were.

Yes, dear.

The slender figure opened her eyes and sat up. And then blinked her eyes in dismay as her gaze passed around the squalid room.

She was on a bed—an iron-framed bed in a small room. On the wall opposite the foot of the bed, and so close that she could all but reach out and touch it, was an old scarred dresser. The room had two doors. The only other furniture besides the bed and dresser were two chairs, one an overstuffed monster in an ill-fitting slip cover, the other a straight-backed chair painted a light brown.

There were two windows, both covered by drawn paper shades. Sunlight spilled through the creases and cracks in the old shades.

The room was stuffy and filled with the stale smells of cigarette smoke, alcohol, and something else which her nose finally identified as the mixed smell of sweat and sex.

She was naked, but she climbed from the bed and raised the shades and then the windows.

The air outside was as still as it was in the small room; it was hot and humid. She struggled to get a full breath of it.

Below were the sounds of midtown traffic. Her windows looked down on a side street clogged with delivery trucks and taxicabs.

One door opened upon a corridor. She gained only the impression of drab brownness before she closed that door again. The other door opened on a shallow closet. Hanging there were the clothes she'd been wearing that long-distant night when the Others had kidnapped her. They were soiled and they smelled. Her nose wrinkled with involuntary disgust.

But then her body went rigid for a long moment, and the room changed. The sunlight seemed to cleave the thick air, burning and cleaning it. A fresh breeze of a fragrance unknown in Manhattan at that time of the year swept out the corners of the room.

The clothes, hung hastily over wire hangers, shimmered briefly. When she took them down they were clean, fresh-smelling. She slipped quickly into them, and then tried the corridor door again.

A faded hall runner of an indiscriminate brown matched the dark brown doors and light brown walls in its depressing drabness. She followed the hall to a single elevator and rang.

When the elevator came, it was run by an old man with a toothless grin and the remnants of long gray hair pressed greasily over his bald pate. His collar was several shades darker than his none-too-clean shirt, and matched by his cuffs.

"You up kinda early today, missy," he said with a vacuous chuckle. She said nothing, but waited in silence for the elevator to complete its descent.

"Thet fella was with you yestidy—he shore stayed a long time, huh? A rich john, huh?"

The door rattled open and she stepped out, leaving the old man perched on his stool, staring hungrily at her retreating backside.

The hotel was on 43rd Street near Times Square, and it was a crib joint; that was obvious. It was also obvious that the Others had not been content to let her body lie fallow. She had been put to work.

She walked around Times Square for a time, her eyes taking in the sights, her ears the sounds, of the noisy but wilted crowds drawn here by some vague sympathetic magic: the promise of the crowds they themselves constituted. Native New Yorkers avoided the area when at all possible. On one corner a man in shirtsleeves and a cardboard hat was hawking sightseeing tours; just down the street another man had set up a sidewalk display of brightly colored mechanical monkeys. Bright-eyed throngs of out-of-town tourists drank up the sights: others like themselves and those who were here to prey upon them.

She ducked into a building entrance. She needed no more of this.

A middle-aged man with too much nose and too little chin came through the doors of the building entrance. "I beg your pardon," he said, as he stepped past the pert brunette, and then he blinked. There was no one there. No one at all.

A startled receptionist looked up. She hadn't heard the door open, but a young woman was standing in front of her.

"Is Mr. Edwards or Mr. Archer in?" the woman asked.

"Do you have an appointment?" the receptionist parried.

The woman shook her head and smiled. "It won't be necessary. I can see they're in." She leaned forward a trifle and lowered her voice. The receptionisht found herself leaning forward, too. "I'd suggest you start hunting a new job. This one won't be lasting much longer."

Then, before the receptionist's startled eyes, the other woman shimmered, and then winked out. The room was empty again.

She stared at the empty space for several moments, her mind numbed by the experience. Then, muttering to herself, she shook her head and turned back to the file cards she'd been sorting. She sorted half a dozen, and then shook her head again. Hesitatingly, she reached for the buzzer. Then, decisively, she pushed it.

"Mr. Edwards?" she said. She waited for a reply.

She waited for a long time.

It had been easy to deal with Edwards and Archer. And Max thought it was particularly fitting that he send them to the same other-dimensional reality to which they'd consigned him: Qanar. He hoped they'd enjoy living out the rest of their mortal life-spans as simple human beings.

They'd not expected him to return; he'd caught them flat-footed. And he'd wasted no time on confrontations or farewells. And so, before they'd had but a momentary awareness of their danger, it was done. They were finished with.

You've won! came Fran's thought.

I've won the battle—but not yet the war, was Max's terse reply.

That is correct. The thought lanced through them with an almost physical shock.

The floor fell away beneath them, and the walls dissolved. The frail body which they both inhabited fell, skirts whipping up over bare thighs, and Max felt her throat muscles contract as Fran screamed.

Steady. He put all his reassurance into that thought, flashing Fran images of the two of them walking arm in arm through a pleasant park glen; the two of them together in Max's apartment, his arms around her, holding her close, their lips touching, meeting...warmth...love. And then it was as though he could almost feel her hand in his, giving him a gentle squeeze.

They were in a great chamber. A single light hung low overhead, illuminating only the small circle in which Fran's body stood. Beyond the circle of illumination sat eight men.

Fran was to remember little of what ensued. It was largely incomprehensible to her, and it was so *fast.* She could retain only blurry images of vast energies unleashed, of mighty strainings over tiny levers and fulcrums, of static faces, impassive, grouped around her still figure.

Later Max left her body and appeared to her in a phantasm.

"I could say that we won because we were on the side of the godly," he said with a grin. He took her hands in his and squeezed them. "But it was simpler than that. They were stunted creatures, Fran—terribly stunted within themselves. They were corrupt, and they'd suffered the ultimate corruption: they were no longer their own masters.

"It had to do with the way they thought. You see, each of them, when he came into his Gift, had formed decisive personality traits, ways of thinking. His Gift didn't change that—it only augmented it.

"They *never* thought of themselves for what they truly were; they never tried to use their vast powers to understand the scheme of things and where in it they fitted. They were content to think of themselves still as human beings with great powers. They never gave any thought to that which lies beyond humanity.

"That's what defeated them in the end. They chose to think of themselves in crippling terms, and they lost a great measure of their powers and abilities for the simple reason that they'd never known they had them—they'd never tried them. And they couldn't. Those powers were incompatible with their stunted thinking."

"And you, Max...?"

"I am what I am, Fran."

"What are you?"

"I am the next step beyond humanity. I am the product of humanity's evolution."

Chapter 19

He explained it to her carefully. He was no longer human. His birthright was the universe. He no longer needed or required a human body. Soon he must depart.

"But...Max. What about ...us?"

"Fran, I love you. You know that. You've felt it. But daily I am growing apart from what you are. And soon I will not be someone you yourself know well enough—to love. Right now I am still only Superman to you. But, don't you see? This body of mine you are holding—it's not real. I made it up for you, to give you a little of the old Max to hold onto."

"What about all the things you could do for the world now? Remember? You had such grand plans. You could end war, hunger, poverty—"

"I've done all I should, Fran. I'm not God, and I'll not play God. The Others—they tampered with people, with human beings, because they had the ability to. It pleased their vanities. Pretty soon they grew contemptuous of humanity. They took delight in manipulating humans in more and more subtle ways, until the humans were themselves manipulating themselves for the Others.

"Humanity is free of the corrupting influence of the Others now. But I don't fully trust myself, Fran. Right now I exist without any exterior discipline. Nothing holds me in check or supplies a balance. And here—in this context, I am a petty god. I could start thinking like one, too, if I let myself.

"No—I'll not tamper with human destinies. Each man and woman must find his own way. Humanity must solve its own problems, if the solutions are to be meaningful. I think you know that, Fran."

He spent that last night with her, and for Fran it was an unforgettably poignant night; the last with Max here on Earth that she would ever know.

They took a final walk in the Park, until the sun rode low in the westward heavens. Then they took a subway train uptown, to the Fort Tryon Park, which had once been a part of the Rockefeller Estate. There they strolled along the terraces which overlooked the Hudson River, and the sun hung over the New Jersey Palisades, its warm golden rays picking out in long shadows the neat rows of low-leafed trees, the garden walks, and the flowers whose fragrance perfumed the heavy air.

They strolled along the terraces and mounted the wide steps to the lookout plaza ringed by trees, and they watched sailboats on the Hudson, and then crossed over to watch the dusk fall over the city, haze hanging low over rooftops, the bright lights of a distant El train picking their way along a steel ribbon.

It was as though she had never seen the city before, and she felt almost as though she would never see it again. But Max was there, close and comforting, his hand in hers, or his arm around her waist, and sometimes she would lean against him and close her eyes, and treasure that most of all.

They slept together a final time that night, and it was almost as though they had embarked upon their honeymoon, the joy and love she felt in giving her body to him, and in drawing him to her.

They awoke late in the morning, the sun streaming thickly through the open windows, catching and holding dancing dust-motes in the still air.

She stretched, arching her back in a feline gesture, and rolled over to look at him. He regarded her from improbably clear blue eyes, and then smiled.

"How would you like breakfast in bed?" he asked, and at her delighted smile, he gestured grandiosely, and she felt the solid thump of a tray across her knees.

She held the tray on her lap and stared softly at him.

"You must go now?"

"I must, Fran. But don't be unhappy. This is not the end for us. You know that—you've felt it too.

"Remember this: every human being carries in him the dormant seeds of evolution. And you—you were with me, in my battle with the Others. I drew upon your own latent powers as well as my own. That may stimulate them."

They ate the breakfast together in close silence, and then Fran put the tray down on the floor beside the bed.

Max leaned toward her, and she surrendered herself to his encircling arms. They kissed.

And then she was alone again. Alone but for the tray. It was a beautiful tray of inlaid teak, and she held it and fingered it for a long time, the memory of that last kiss still upon her lips.

CHAPTER TWENTY

That night Francine had trouble falling asleep. But finally she did, still tossing and turning against a sweat-soaked sheet.

And, later in the night, she dreamed strange dreams...and she floated five inches above her bed.

About the Author:

Ted White is a multiple Hugo Award nominee and winning writer/editor. A long-time SF fan, he first entered the field professionally in 1962 as a collaborator on a series of science fiction and fantasy stories and novels written with such notables as Marion Zimmer Bradley, Terry Carr and Dave Van Arnam and as an assistant editor at *F&SF*. His major novels include *The Jewels of Elsewhen, No Time Like Tomorrow* and *The Great Gold Steal.* It was the decade that he put in as editor of *Amazing* and *Fantastic* magazines which earned him the most attention—not only via his controversial and very personal editorials but through the lively and distinguished fiction which he filled its pages. After a brief stint as editor of *Heavy Metal,* he has returned to his ancestral home in Falls Church, Virginia to resume his career as a writer.